ONE EASY S... WOULD HAVE ENDED THE CHARADE ONCE AND FOR ALL...

The outlaw masquerading as the Indian ghost had shown himself to be cunning and cruel. Slocum wasn't going to underestimate him now. Every sense alert to the slightest motion, sound or presence, Slocum entered the barn, gun barrel swiveling left and right. Only the sounds from the horses came to him. He advanced searching each stall, left and right, as he went to be sure he hadn't been mistaken about which one the ghost hid in.

Approaching the stall where he'd last seen the ghost, Slocum spun and held the cocked Colt in front of him, ready to fire.

He didn't believe what he saw...

OTHER BOOKS BY JAKE LOGAN

JAKE LOGAN

SLOCUM AND
THE INDIAN GHOST

BERKLEY BOOKS, NEW YORK

SLOCUM AND THE INDIAN GHOST

A Berkley Book/published by arrangement with
the author

PRINTING HISTORY
Berkley edition/December 1986

ISBN: 0-425-09395-6

A BERKLEY BOOK ® TM 757,375
Berkley Books are published by The Berkley Publishing Group,
200 Madison Avenue, New York, N.Y. 10016.
The name "BERKLEY" and the stylized "B" with design are
trademarks belonging to Berkley Publishing Corporation.

PRINTED IN THE UNITED STATES OF AMERICA

1

John Slocum had been in San Francisco for over two
months. That was a long time for him to stay in any one
place, but the poker games along the Embarcadero had
been damned good to him. The winter winds of '88 had
blown him into the seaport flat busted from a stretch of bad
luck tin panning for gold in half-frozen streams in the
Sierra Madres, and he'd found any number of sailors who
didn't know odds like he did—and who couldn't keep their
faces expressionless when they looked at their cards.

Spring and a pocket filled with greenbacks made him
feel itchy and ready to move on, after just one more night
in Irish Mike's Saloon working those with more money
than good sense.

"How many?" demanded a half-drunk, belligerent,

ruddy-faced sailor sitting at the beer-stained table across from Slocum. Slocum stretched his rangy six-foot frame, then settled back in such a way that no one noticed that his left hand rested closer to his vest pocket than to the cards. A two-shot derringer weighed down a watch pocket. Slocum shook his head slightly, indicating he'd stand pat. Why draw to a full house, queens over fours?

"You don't want none?" the sailor asked, squinting like a boar pig ready to charge. Even from across the table, the man's sour breath made Slocum draw back slightly.

"I like these," Slocum said, his fingers curling around the ebony handle of the small gun. His green eyes darted to the others seated and waiting at the table. They all appeared high-strung and jumpy, like thoroughbreds pawing at the dirt and ready for a race to start. Two were sailors from the same ship as his drunken opponent. The other three smiled almost wickedly.

Slocum liked their looks even less than he did the drunk sailor's. Those three might be crimps preying on the unsuspecting and incautious. They roved the dockside taverns until they found a man so far lost in his cups that he couldn't stand without help; he'd come to his senses, hung over and on his way to Hong Kong. Or maybe they'd help him along with a bottle of cheap Billy Taylor's whiskey laced with enough opium to stun a grizzly. Slocum knew the crimps weren't even above prowling the crowded San Francisco streets in broad daylight using hung-shot blackjacks to meet their quotas.

From the talk that had gone around Irish Mike's earlier, Slocum knew that no fewer than three China Clippers had docked, and all needed replacements for crewmen who had died during passage or had gained their freedom by jumping ship.

"Dealer takes three," said the sailor. His bloodshot eyes

widened slightly as he stared at his new hand. Slocum watched the predictable emotions come and go like the San Francisco Bay tides. It didn't take an experienced player to realize that the sailor had nothing worth betting, and that he would try running a bluff because he was too drunk to give in without a fight.

Slocum decided to end this and get out of the saloon before everything exploded and he was caught in the middle.

"Five hundred," Slocum said, pushing his entire pile of greenbacks forward. He watched the sailor's face go slack, then harden into a mask of sullen anger.

"I don't have that much," the sailor said.

"Then the pot's mine. House rules. You can't ante, you fold." Slocum reached for the pile of money on the table with his right hand even as he drew the deadly derringer and cocked it under the table with his left.

The sailor roared in anger and blasted to his feet, kicking back his rickety chair and shoving the table hard into Slocum's belly. Slocum cursed. The impact of the table against his arm caused him to lose his grip on the tiny gun. It clattered to the floor, the sound of its accidental discharge lost in the swell of angry voices.

A brawl had started the instant the sailor got to his feet. On Slocum's left, one of the men he'd thought to be a crimp pulled out a long, slender canvas bag filled with lead shot—his black jack. One quick swing with that formidable weapon sent one sailor tumbling unconscious to the floor. The other two shanghaiers jumped another sailor and wrestled him to the ground.

Then Slocum became too busy to notice those around him. A fist toughened by hard work and salt water crashed into the side of his face, sending him reeling back. Slocum sprawled awkwardly, the impact on the sawdust-covered floor almost knocking the wind from him. He managed to bring his knees up to his chest in time to catch the burly sailor. A powerful thrust of his legs sent the sailor crashing into those behind him. Slocum rolled to the side and came to his feet, the Colt from his cross-draw holster in his hand. He had a clear shot at the sailor, but Slocum hesitated. He wasn't going to shoot the man in the back. The drunken sailor had become tangled up with three others who were swinging fists and shouting curses at the top of their lungs.

Slocum slumped when someone hit him from behind. Somehow he managed to hang onto the Colt as he dropped to his knees. Through the ringing in his ears, he heard a distant voice say, ". . . a good one. We can get an easy hundred for him. Have Pierre drag 'im out!"

Slocum tried to stand but found only deadness in his legs. The blow to the base of his spine had paralyzed him. He looked up to see two men gliding at the edge of the fight, polished wooden clubs swinging now and then onto exposed backs or heads. The crimps would have a full quota soon at this rate.

Working against the pain of returning sensation in his back and legs, Slocum dragged himself to one side. The Colt stayed firmly in his hand. It would take more than a shanghaier to get him. Endless months at sea working for stale bread and wormy jerky wasn't the way he wanted to spend the rest of his life. As long as he had the Colt, they wouldn't take him.

The sailor who had started the fight surged up from the bottom of a pile of men. Arms and legs seemed to explode in every direction. The sailor bellowed like a whale surfacing. Those meaty fists began swinging methodically, each blow sending a man to the floor. The way one crimp's head snapped back told Slocum that the sailor had broken the man's neck with a single punch.

"Where's that son of a bitch what tried to rob me?" the sailor cried. Slocum didn't have any doubt who the man wanted. He began worrying that even his Colt might not be enough to stop this seafaring mountain of muscle and drunken madness.

Like a fish out of water, Slocum flopped around and got to the other side of a post supporting the roof. It wasn't enough to hide him from the sailor's view, but it provided a crutch firm enough to help Slocum stand. Slocum began staggering toward the door on wobbly legs. He grunted when someone struck him just above the right knee and sent him back to the floor.

"Enough of this," Slocum muttered to himself. The man who had collided with him was out cold, a large bruise already forming in the center of his forehead from a crimp's blackjack.

"You!" came the cry. "You tried to cheat me!"

Slocum painfully got to his feet and faced the sailor. The ruddy face had turned even darker from a nasty cut over the sailor's left eye. The blood flowing in a steady stream must have blinded him in one eye, but the determined, drunken man didn't seem to notice.

"I'm gonna rip your damned arms off for tryin' to cheat me!"

Slocum had less than a second to make his decision. He didn't cotton to the idea of shooting an unarmed man. He liked the idea of that sailor ripping off his arms even less. Slocum raised his Colt and fired in a smooth, well-oiled movement. The roar from the pistol caused a momentary silence to fall in the saloon.

Then the fight started again, this time in earnest. Slocum glanced over at the sailor, who clutched his shattered leg and swore a blue streak. His bloodshot eyes squinted at

Slocum with hatred so pure that it burned like an alcohol flame. Slocum considered putting a second bullet into the man's thick, shaggy-haired head and taking care of a passel of problems. Being a poor loser at cards was one thing, but a poor loser carrying a grudge was another. Slocum never liked having anyone trailing along behind him who wasn't inclined to be at least a bit on the friendly side. To have this burly galoot dogging his steps wasn't something Slocum wanted to consider.

"I should shoot you," he said as he walked over to the sailor. "But I don't want to waste the ammunition." Slocum kicked the fallen man in the belly as hard as he could. The sailor folded over like a closing jackknife and went out like a light.

Slocum picked up what money he could find on the floor. It was all his winnings. He smiled slightly when he saw the sailor's cards lying in a neat stack on the floor, still face down. On impulse he turned them over. It was as he'd thought: The man had drawn three and got shit to go with a pair of treys.

Even with the din of a full-fledged saloon fight going on around him, something warned Slocum of danger. He ducked into a low crouch and had his Colt out and aimed. Behind him stood one of the shanghaiers, a bloody club in his hands.

For an instant their eyes locked. Slocum's cold gaze wore the other man down. The crimp smiled weakly and said, "Sorry, friend. Thought you was somebody else."

All around him, the team of crimps worked to get rid of those who had fallen in the fight. Most of the sailors would find themselves stripped naked and taken to new ships. To them it would hardly matter what master they sailed under. A few others being dragged out were local men who had been hanging out in the saloon when the fight started.

Slocum got to his feet and backed away. The crimp eyed him as if he were a side of dressed-out beef—and, to a man such as this, that was all he was. Slocum fought down his revulsion for the man and his unsavory profession. Back in Georgia before the War, Slocum's family had never been slaveholders and hadn't taken kindly to those who were. His father had always held that a man valued everything he worked for personally, and that gain from the struggles of a slave made you something less than a man. Slocum had fought under the banner of the Stars and Bars more out of dedication to his home than for the institution of slavery. And while all the War and the following Reconstruction had brought him was suffering, loss of family and farm, and a price on his head for killing a thieving carpetbagger judge, Slocum still had no good feelings for slavery of any kind.

What the crimps did with the drunks and unfortunates they caught was no different than what the antebellum Southern cotton farmers had done with their black men and women. But Slocum was no fool and held back his emotions. To begin a gunfight against this well-organized band would spell his own death.

Slocum staggered from the saloon and into the chilly, damp San Francisco night. A strong spring breeze blew in off the Bay and cut to the bone. Slocum pulled his broadcloth coat tighter around him and thrust cold hands into his pockets. The left pocket overflowed with greenbacks still damp with sweat and blood. In the right rested his Colt. He had no idea what had happened to the small derringer; it was on the saloon floor, and it could damn well stay there for all he cared. He was away from the fight and once more free.

He turned into the wind and followed it until he came to the edge of the water. The scent of fish rotting made Slocum wrinkle his nose. He preferred the clean, sharp scent of high country pines or the tangy odor of horses and tack.

Slocum turned and looked back toward the saloon perched halfway up the hill. The door stood ajar and occasional dark figures moved across the light coming from inside. He didn't need an owl's eyesight to know that the crimps were still at work. Before they were done, there wouldn't be a single patron left inside.

Faint snippets of conversation drifted to him, some words garbled by the wind. "... somewhere toward the water. Son of ..."

Slocum settled his nerves until his hand was rock-steady. He rubbed the back of his leg where he'd been hit, then worked up, kneading knotted, bruised muscles until he came to the small of his back. He almost fainted from the jolt of pain this light touch produced. The crimp had been expert at aiming. Slocum knew it would be quite a while before he could walk without feeling the pain here.

"Time to get the hell out of San Francisco," he muttered. Slocum straightened and took another deep breath. When he felt better he started along the shoreline, heading west. He had been staying at a small rooming house not far from the docks. Once there, he might rest for the night, get a horse the next morning, and head south.

Slocum hadn't gone fifty paces when he heard a soft, feminine voice call, "Psst! Hey, mister. Wait. Please. I need help!"

Slocum stopped and listened hard before moving. He heard nothing to alert him: no running feet, no harsh breathing, no scrape of gunmetal against leather.

"Here, please. Over here!"

Slocum turned and slowly went to the shadow-darkened doorway. A faint beam of moonlight caught the woman's face and highlighted it. It made her look like Satan's hand-maiden.

"They're after me. I need help, mister."

"Who?"

"The crimps. They want me."

"Nobody would shanghai a woman," Slocum said, suspicions flaring.

Long years as being the hunter gave Slocum enough insight into what the prey felt like to let him know that someone stalked him now. He ducked just as a heavy canvas bag filled with sand crunched into the doorjamb inches above his head.

"Git him, you danged fool!" the woman shrieked. She came at Slocum, knobby fingers hooked like talons. She raked at his face, but Slocum had learned his lesson. He moved fast and kept moving. Pain lanced through him as he twisted around to face the man with the blackjack. Slocum felt powerful arms encircle his body and begin to squeeze. He wondered if oak staves felt like this when the hot iron bands were fastened to make a rain barrel.

"Thass it, Luke. Squeeze the son of a bitch senseless!"

Slocum wanted to cry out in anger, but he found that the strong arms prevented him from sucking in much-needed air. Every time he exhaled, he came that much closer to blacking out. Reaching the end of his rope, survival outweighed all else.

His hand had closed on the butt of his Colt just as the giant of a man's arms pinned him. Slocum pulled the trigger, not knowing or much caring where the barrel pointed. The normally loud report was muffled by his assailant's belly. The man grunted and the crushing force of his arms fell away.

Slocum hit the pavement and dropped to his knees,

smoking gun still in hand. A second shot wasn't necessary. Luke lay flat on his back, sightless, staring eyes catching the dim moonbeams and turning them into silver.

"Luke?" the woman asked, her voice choked. "You all right, Luke? You stupid bastard, you can't die on me. Luke!"

She knelt beside the mountain of a man and cradled his head in her lap. Slocum said nothing as he got to his feet and backed off. He'd had enough of the San Francisco waterfront. Crimps looking for victims to sell to Orient-bound sea captains. Drunken sailors. Poor losers. Cheap whores and backshooting sneak thieves. The idea of riding south toward Los Gatos and maybe even farther than that appealed to him more and more.

Slocum holstered his Colt when he'd gone another block. After he'd gone another two, he felt good about his decision to take his hard-won poker earnings and find less populated areas. He didn't fit into San Francisco society. Too many people jostled his elbow. Too many wanted nothing more than to rob him. Slocum had done a bit of that in his day to stay alive, but these people were professionals. Day in, day out, they stole and killed.

Some even did it because of a sick thrill they got from it. Slocum understood killing. Long years ago during the War he had been a sniper and a damned good one. He would sit on a ridge and wait for the sun to glint off a Union officer's shiny gold braid. Without their officers, the Yankees had a harder time mounting a battle. Slocum had been personally responsible for quite a few Confederate victories because of his sharp eye and sharper shooting.

He was no stranger to killing, but never had he killed wantonly, even when he rode with Quantrill and Bloody Bill Anderson. War was one thing, self-defense another.

Those butchers cared nothing for either. They just enjoyed killing.

Slocum was no stranger to death. That didn't make it any easier for him to accept the way things were done in San Francisco.

His body still hurting but his spine straighter now that he'd reached the decision to leave the city for less populated parts, he walked briskly back to the boarding house.

At dawn's first pearly gray and pink light, John Slocum was riding south, four hundred and eighty-seven dollars in greenbacks rustling in his saddlebag.

2

The wind in his face carried the odor of sweet, growing plants forcing their way up through dry soil to a spring sun. Slocum inhaled deeply. This was a vast improvement over the stench of fish floating belly-up in San Francisco Bay, and over the stale interiors of too many saloons that had blurred in his mind. He belonged outdoors, away from the crush of people all wanting something from him, free, where he could roam as he saw fit.

"There, there, old girl," he said, patting the strawberry roan on the neck. "No need to get spooked." The horse continued to prance about, as if she heard something that Slocum hadn't.

The man had learned to trust the senses of animals, sometimes more than his own. He'd heard it said that this area had earthquakes now and again, one not six years back in '82, and that the dogs and horses sensed the deep inner rumblings long before any human felt them. Slocum doubted they were in for another earthquake, but other problems might be brewing all around.

His sharp eyes scanned the road ahead. Empty. He swiveled in the saddle and stood up in his stirrups, wincing slightly at the pang in his back. No one followed him. He heaved a sigh of relief at this. All night long he'd had nightmares of men chasing him with clubs, wanting to shanghai him. Worst of all, in his nightmare they'd caught him and sent him out to a boat whose captain was the sailor he'd shot.

The ruddy-faced sailor had reared up ten feet tall and laughed, his fetid breath hot in Slocum's face. Slocum had awakened in a cold sweat, hand already halfway toward the Colt hung on the back of a chair near the bed.

Slocum settled down in the worn saddle and tried to tell himself that the only thing wrong was his case of nerves. As he rode, though, the sense of being watched mounted until he got the twitches. Slocum hadn't stayed alive as long as he had by ignoring his feelings.

He jerked the roan's reins to the left and got off the road. The dusty Salinas Valley road wasn't heavily traveled this time of year. The farmers trying to eke out their miserable existences in the dryness worked long hours at their crop irrigation. Most other traffic north and south either went on ships along the coast or on the Central Pacific Railroad spur line twenty miles to the east through San Jose.

Slocum cut back and forth through stands of scrubby trees and undergrowth, back to the deeply rutted road, then across to the other side. All the while, he listened hard and tried to see what it was riling him and his horse.

He saw nothing.

"Whoever's out there is damned good," he muttered to himself. "Or I might be imagining it all."

Slocum laughed and put his heels solidly into the roan's flanks. That was as good an explanation as any. No one followed him. He'd made sure of that. If this unseen tracker worked alongside the road keeping pace with Slocum and out of sight at the same time, he was as good as the best Indian scout Slocum had ever encountered.

Still, Slocum couldn't shake the uneasy feeling of eyes on him as he rode along.

At midday he stopped to eat and give the roan a well-deserved rest. As he worked on a plate of beans and a can of peaches, Slocum came alert. His hand flashed to the butt of his Colt slung in his cross-draw holster. The sound had been so slight that it might have been nothing more than a rabbit slipping through underbrush. Slocum didn't think so. It was early spring, but the unusual heat in the valley approached desert temperatures. No animal would be venturing forth now; they'd wait till sundown to forage or hunt.

Unless the animal walked on two legs. Road agents weren't likely to worry about how hot it was if they sniffed after a victim.

Slocum rose and moved silently, circling his temporary camp in ever-widening circles. Once he found a low jacaranda bush with a freshly broken twig at ankle level. Other than this, he found no spoor of his mysterious watcher.

Frowning, he returned to his interrupted noon meal. That someone tracked him Slocum had no doubt. But why?

The money in his saddlebag would prove a mighty big reason, he knew. Had someone from San Francisco followed him all this way to rob him, or was he just running counter to a local road agent? Either way, Slocum didn't like it.

The unseen man out in the stunted undergrowth was too damned good. A single mistake with this man and Slocum knew he would end up as buzzard meat.

"Let's get on our way," Slocum said to his horse. He had rubbed the animal down and let her graze a little. The dry countryside hadn't given up any water for her, but he knew that a small tributary to a bigger river flowed nearby. Slocum wondered if he should try to find it or simply press on and try to reach Los Gatos, which couldn't be more than a couple hours' easy ride.

The matter was settled for him when he swung up into the saddle. The snap of a rifle and the whine of its bullet came almost at the same time. Slocum felt a hot streak cross his shoulder blades. He fell forward over the saddle pommel, more in startled reaction than in pain.

Bending low, he kicked the roan into a gallop. He wasn't in any condition for a fight with a man who drifted like a ghost through the countryside and shot with such deadly accuracy. Whoever this road agent was, he knew the terrain well. As Slocum raced on, he caught no sight of the bushwhacker.

A mile down the road, the shallow wound began to hurt like hell. Two miles and it felt as if a hill of fire ants had taken nest and burrowed into his flesh. Like it or not, Slocum had to rein in and eventually come to a halt. The hot sun burning down made him sweat, and the salty sweat poured into his shoulder wound.

"Enough of this. Go for the water," he told his horse. The strawberry roan tossed her head and whinnied, then turned to the left and obediently trotted off. Slocum gave the animal her head. Within five minutes, they stood on the bank of a sluggishly flowing stream choked with winter debris.

Slocum wasted no time. He pulled off his gunbelt and, keeping the Colt firmly in his left hand, turned around and sat down heavily on the muddy bank. He fell backward. The water seemed to rip at his wound and threatened to make him pass out. He hung on, refusing to give in to such minor pain. He'd experienced worse than this and lived through it.

By the time the river had washed off the worst of the dried blood, Slocum began peeling off his shirt clumsily with his right hand. Even so, pulling it away from the shallow wound made him think a flaming arrow had been dragged across his shoulders.

He cleaned off his damaged shirt as best he could, then awkwardly tended to his wound. His arms refused to bend in the proper places to do more than a crude job. Bandaging the wound was out of the question. Slocum had to content himself with sitting by the river and waiting for the blood to clot again.

"Not more'n a scratch and it hurts like a house afire," he complained. The horse barely listened to him, more interested in drinking her fill. Slocum heaved himself to his feet and pulled the reluctant horse from the stream. He didn't want her bloating. Taking care of his own problems seemed more than he could handle.

Slocum stretched slowly, testing the limits of his movement. He couldn't do much more than lift his arms shoulder high before the pain flashed across his back. With the still-sore bruise he'd received at the small of his back from the shanghai-minded crimp, he wasn't in the best condition for a fight.

But John Slocum wasn't about to let any road agent

shoot him down like a dog. The hunted would become the hunter.

The only problem Slocum had was deciding how to do this. Even before he'd been shot, he hadn't been able to find his tracker. The thought that the road agent might be a renegade Indian entered his mind and left it almost immediately. Other parts of the country had Indian trouble, not California. The Mescalero and Jicarilla Apaches were in Arizona and New Mexico. The Utes had been quiet for some time in Colorado and Utah. And no trouble at all had surfaced in California. Slocum saw no reason to believe a single renegade from any of the more warlike tribes had come this far west simply to bedevil him.

"Who the hell's out there?" Slocum wondered. He didn't think any white man could elude him for long, yet this one had, and was doing a good job of keeping out of sight.

Slocum put his damp shirt back on, shuddering slightly at the feel of the cloth against his wound. In a few seconds the hint of discomfort faded and he was ready to ride.

"Los Gatos?" he asked the roan. The horse shook her head. "I agree. We go after that damned road agent." He brought the horse around and backtracked carefully. With luck, he'd find the bushwhacker before the man found him.

Luck proved elusive for Slocum. By sunset he'd seen two farms in the hazy distance but no sign that another rode along stalking him. Slocum would have thought it all a figment of his imagination except for the bullet wound burning like acid across his shoulders.

Slocum made camp for the night beneath a tree, taking care to leave his bedroll in such a fashion that the guttering flames made it seem as if a man slept within. Slocum perched in the vee of a cottonwood tree a few yards distant, his hand on his holstered Colt. All night long he dozed, more alert than asleep. When the first rays of dawn teased his eyelids, he came fully awake, stiff and aching.

He dropped to the ground and stretched tired muscles. He had slept but hadn't rested in the tree.

Slocum ate a small, cold breakfast, not wanting to take more time than necessary to be on the road again. He snorted in the cool morning air and shook himself until the last of the aches had vanished. Whoever had hunted him the previous day had given up the chase. Why? Slocum decided that the answer to that might come in the same breath as the answer to who tracked him.

He mounted and took a few minutes to survey the landscape. All the running around the day before had taken him farther west than he'd intended. Los Gatos lay more to the south and east now, putting him closer to San Jose. Slocum shrugged. One town was as good as the other, as far as he was concerned.

"Just so long as there's nobody shooting at me," he said.

Slocum rode slowly, his body protesting every time the horse jolted him. But he smiled more now. The springtime worked its magic on him. He had money in his saddlebag and hard times were past. What more could a man want?

Slocum tried to quiet the roan when she spooked, but he was momentarily unbalanced. When the rifle shot rang out, the horse stumbled and then began to run.

"Whoa!" Slocum shouted. He pulled hard at the reins and slowly regained control. But the horse's gait began to change in a way that Slocum didn't like. By the time he had guided the animal toward a small stand of trees, the roan was staggering.

When the animal dropped forward, head down, she sent Slocum tumbling. Slocum hit and rolled the best he could.

He came around, hand on his gun. For a moment, he knelt in the dust, speechless. The road agent—he had no reason to believe this was a different one—had shot and killed his horse.

The animal thrashed about, then gave a final convulsive kick and lay still. Slocum scuttled over and laid a hand on the horse's neck. No strong heartbeat vibrated the flesh. A single eye peered at the sky and already began to mist over with death.

"You stinking son of a bitch!" Slocum shouted. "Show yourself! Fight like a man, goddamn you!"

Another rifle shot took Slocum's hat off his head. He ducked down behind the carcass of his horse and lay there seething. This road agent intended to kill him and steal what he could, that was obvious. Equally obvious, the bandit was cunning, one damn fine tracker, and able to hit what he aimed at with his rifle.

Slocum cursed anew when he saw that the roan had fallen in such a way to pin his own rifle between ground and horse. He'd have to make do with his Colt.

He reached up to unfasten his saddlebag and was greeted by four quick rifle shots that drove him back to cover. Slocum realized he couldn't stay behind the horse forever. A slight shift in position, perhaps to higher ground, and the sniper would have a perfect shot at him. Slocum peered around the horse's flank and carefully studied the low ridge running along the road. He knew the sniper had to be there because that was where *he* would be if their positions were reversed.

A sudden glint of sunlight off a shiny barrel confirmed his guess. Knowing the road agent's location enabled him to choose the best path to the stand of trees he had vainly tried to reach on horseback.

He gathered his feet under him, then erupted, his lanky

frame twisting and turning to confuse the sniper. Although several bullets sang through the air inches away, his tactic worked. Slocum dived behind a fallen tree and lay gasping for breath—but safe.

For the moment.

Slocum didn't rest long. He had to keep moving or the road agent would pot him like a tin can on a fence post. Slocum went deeper into the copse, then began circling around. He knew the road agent had to come down from that ridge if he wanted the saddlebag on the dead horse. When he did, Slocum would be waiting.

"Damn you," Slocum muttered. He heard another horse but the sniper didn't come directly to the fallen roan. Instead, the man circled, knowing Slocum awaited him with cocked pistol.

Slocum refused to be outflanked. He kept moving until he found a spot behind a boulder that gave adequate protection to his back and allowed him a shot of less than fifty yards should the bushwhacker come to take his spoils. It would be a tricky shot with a handgun, but Slocum thought he was up to it.

"Just to line that son of a bitch up in my sights," he said. "You killed a good horse and now you're going to pay for it."

Again Slocum misjudged the other man's ability and cunning. A bullet richocheted off the top of the boulder behind which he hid—and the bullet had come from his left. Slocum hurriedly slipped around, Colt ready for action.

Just for an instant he saw a flash of red-and-black-checked flannel shirt. Slocum fired and even as the heavy recoil slammed the gun back into his hand, he knew he'd missed. There hadn't been a clean sight picture. He hadn't even had a good look at the road agent.

It was as if Slocum fought a ghost.

Slocum peered around and saw nothing. Cautiously, he slid around the boulder and surveyed the terrain he had just crossed. The whinny of a horse alerted him. He kept moving and stared out at a figure hunched over his fallen roan. The road agent worked to untie the saddlebag containing the greenbacks.

Slocum's heart speeded up until the blood throbbed in his temples. He'd starved all winter in the Sierras panning for gold that didn't exist. He'd played poker in every dive in San Francisco for two months, starting with less than a dollar and ending up with almost five hundred. The fight the night before had reduced his stake a little, but he still had well over four hundred.

The road agent wasn't going to get a damned cent of it!

Slocum lifted his Colt, sighted easily, and fired. Even as the bullet sped on its way, he knew the distance was too great. He'd missed by several feet. Unhurried, the road agent leafed through the thick wad of greenbacks and stuffed them inside his shirt.

Slocum tried to get a good look at the thief. Failing that, he fired again and again, each shot missing its mark. Slocum emptied the revolver and reloaded. By this time, the road agent had unlimbered his rifle and hefted it, getting Slocum in his sights.

Slocum jerked around and went into a crouch behind a pile of gravel. The bandit's slug tore through the loose rock and sent chips flying into Slocum's face. He wiped away blood from half a dozen insignificant scratches that made him even madder.

Slocum dived flat onto his belly and kept firing. One of his slugs came close to the bandit, but other than disturbing his aim for an instant, the man showed no sign of being upset. He fired his Winchester repeatedly, with expert rhythm and ease, levering in one cartridge after another and keeping Slocum pinned down.

Slocum saw he was outgunned at this distance and any real fight would only end in his death.

He made his way back toward the stand of trees, knowing this would give him a better chance to fight.

A rifle bullet took the toe off his right boot and sent him tumbling forward to land flat on his belly. The air gushed from Slocum's lungs and stunned him.

Through blurred eyes he saw the road agent getting back onto his horse. The man lifted his rifle and aimed carefully. As good a shot as the man was, Slocum knew he wouldn't miss. Not this time. Not when it meant removing a witness to his crime.

John Slocum tensed for the bullet that would take his life.

3

John Slocum waited for the bullet that would take his life, but it didn't come. He sucked in a lungful of air, winced at the pain it caused, then got to his hands and knees.

Slocum tried to figure out why the road agent hadn't finished him when he had the chance. Leaving behind an angry victim wasn't smart, and the robber had proven clever up to this point. The man had put away his rifle and jerked hard at the reins to get his horse turned and running down the road. Slocum got to his feet and fired quickly five times. The sixth time the hammer fell on an empty chamber. It didn't matter. With a cartridge in the chamber, Slocum hadn't come close enough to the robber to scare him.

Slocum began reloading, but by the time all six shells

had slipped home, hardly a cloud of dust remained to mark the road agent's passage.

Dejected, Slocum stalked out to his roan. A cloud of iridescent blue and green flies took to wing as he disturbed their meal. His nose wrinkled at the odor of decaying flesh. The horse hadn't lasted long in the hot noonday sun.

"You're going to pay for this," Slocum promised the vanished road agent. But his threat rang hollow. The highwayman had taken his money, killed his horse, and left him in the middle of nowhere with a right boot that had had the end shot off. Slocum wiggled his toes and saw them through the hole.

Somebody would pay for this, but who? Slocum rummaged through his saddlebag and found little that would help him. The robber had even taken the spare box of cartridges. All the ammunition Slocum had was in his gunbelt —fewer than twenty rounds.

"Sorry, old girl," Slocum said, patting the horse on the neck. The once vibrant, living flesh was now a carcass offering a free meal to flies and buzzards. Slocum frowned. Why hadn't the road agent taken the shot that would have left his human victim in a similar condition?

The faint rumble of light, uneven wagon wheels came to Slocum's ears. He spun and peered toward the north. A small dust cloud appeared, one the robber must have seen. Slocum decided that if the sight had driven off the bushwhacker, it could only be good for him. He worked to free his saddle and took the rest of his gear off the fallen roan. His rifle seemed none the worse for having been pinned under the animal's dead bulk. By the time the buckboard came into sight, Slocum was sitting on the saddle beside the road.

"Some things are improving for me," he said when he saw the buckboard's driver. Slocum stood and waved to the young woman sitting primly on the hard wooden seat. She reined in, obviously unsure whether to keep driving or to stop.

She made up her mind and stopped.

"Ma'am," Slocum said, tipping his hat. He saw her brown eyes widen. He knew he looked like he'd been pulled through a knothole backward, but most folks in this part of the country couldn't look much better. There wasn't that much water for daily bathing.

"Your hat," the woman stammered. "It's got a hole in it. A bullet hole!"

Slocum reached up and touched the hole the road agent had put in it. He smiled slowly. He'd forgotten about it.

"Sorry to disturb you like that, ma'am. Didn't remember I had a hole in my hat. Lots else on my mind. My horse . . . died. Can I get a ride with you into San Jose?"

"Died?"

"Road agent," he said, his voice taking on a harsher tone. "He shot my horse out from under me. Put the hole in my hat, too."

"Oh!" The woman put one slender-fingered hand to her lips when he turned slightly. "You're hurt. Let me help you!"

Slocum blinked. He had forgotten that the long, shallow, oozing bullet wound across his broad shoulder blades was visible through the tear in his tattered shirt.

"Doesn't bother me none," Slocum said. He grunted as he hefted his gear and heaved it into the back of the buckboard. Two carpetbags and a small trunk were already there—not much for a young woman traveling any distance across California.

"Name's John Slocum," he said by way of introduction.

"Are you sure you're all right?" she asked. Her brown eyes still stared at his wound.

"Ma'am, I'm *not* all right. I've been shot and robbed and had my horse killed. Does that sound as if I'm all right?"

"I'm sorry," she said, dropping her eyes and putting her hands together primly in her lap. The thick, soft folds of her light tan gingham dress seemed to devour those fine hands. Slocum couldn't help noticing how lovely she was, the firm thrust of breasts against her dress, the trim waist, the swanlike neck and finely formed oval face. She had a small nose with a bewitching upturn at the tip. Slocum wished he could look at her all day long.

She lifted her gaze and tried to smile. It wasn't successful. "I'm not used to all this," she said in a weak voice. "I . . . I've come from San Francisco to take a position with Mrs. Winchester."

"Winchester?" Slocum asked.

"Sarah Winchester. Her husband invented that." The woman pointed at the Winchester Model '73 that Slocum had worked free from under his dead horse. He stared at it, not understanding exactly what the woman meant. "William Winchester. He was Mrs. Winchester's husband. Back East, before he died."

"She lives in these parts?" Slocum had heard nothing about it, but then he had little interest in such matters. Somewhere he had heard that William Winchester had died from tuberculosis six or eight years back, somewhere in the East. Boston, Slocum thought. "Why'd his widow come all the way out here?"

The woman shook her head, then lifted her hand to her lips again in a gesture of horror. "You must think I'm a perfectly awful person. Rude," she said, her voice hardly more than a whisper. "I'm Florabelle Jackson."

"Actually, Miss Jackson, I don't think you're terrible at all. Truth to tell, I was right pleased to see you drive up when you did. It's a long walk into San Jose."

"Only about ten miles. That's not much for a man of your station," the small brunette said without thinking. When she realized how it sounded, she made the gesture of shock at her own stupidity again. "I didn't mean that. I mean . . . oh, it's awful!"

She bent forward, her face in her cupped hands. Slocum swung up onto the buckboard seat beside the woman. He placed a hesitant hand on her quaking shoulder. "There's nothing wrong. You didn't offend me, Miss Jackson. I surely do appreciate what you're doing for me."

"I'm sorry," she repeated. "It . . . it's not you. I didn't mean to make light of your dilemma or cast aspersion on your undoubtedly fine character."

"Are *you* in some kind of trouble? Anything I can help out with?" Slocum figured he couldn't be in any worse shape than he was in. He'd been broke and on foot before, and probably would be again. But something about Florabelle Jackson told him that she was used to only the finer things in life. Those finer things seemed to have been lost somewhere along the road from San Francisco.

The brunette straightened and wiped tears from the corner of her eyes. "I am sorry, sir. Oh, there I go again, apologizing when there's no need. You have been set upon by a thief and I carry on at such lengths about my own insignificant distresses."

"Miss Jackson . . . it is Miss, isn't it?"

"It is, Mr. Slocum."

Her primness almost made Slocum laugh. Out here on the dusty road it seemed out of place. He would have expected this sort of behavior at a fancy society tea up on Nob Hill. Slocum sensed a deep undercurrent of true pain in the beautiful young woman, however, and kept back his laughter.

"Miss Jackson, we look to be two of a kind," he said.

"How's that, sir?" She took the reins and snapped them, to no effect. The tired, swayback mare peered over a knobby shoulder and glared, not moving. Silently, Slocum reached over and took the reins from Florabelle. He "giddyapped" and the horse decided to move. Slowly, to be sure, but it moved.

"Well, Miss Jackson, you've heard the long and short of my trouble. But you, your troubles are brand new."

Florabelle Jackson said nothing. She sat staring straight ahead at the road. Slocum studied her out of the corner of his eye and saw the small muscular twitches that told him he'd hit the nail on the head. He plowed on with his guesses.

"Your family hit upon hard times, didn't they?"

"They died, sir. Rounding the Cape. The *Sea Warrior* sank without a trace. A sister ship's captain claimed it was during the height of a terrible winter storm."

"You reckon it was otherwise?"

"Sir, it was then summer in the Southern Hemisphere. But it no longer matters what I think. Whether the *Sea Warrior* was sacrificed to save another vessel or not is of little importance. My parents, two brothers, and a sister were lost. Along with them went all the family belongings. I am left a pauper."

Slocum guessed that the family fortune had been a modest one, nothing to rival that of the railroad magnates like Leland Stanford.

"So you're cast out into the world on your own, penniless and without anywhere to turn."

"Your tone is mocking, Mr. Slocum."

It was Slocum's turn to apologize. He had lost his entire family and farm when he was hardly older than Florabelle, and this had happened after he'd endured life-threatening injuries and the continual promise of violent, bloody death offered by the War. He might have had it harder reaching this point in his life, but that was no reason to criticize Florabelle or to poke fun at her loss.

"Your apology is accepted, Mr. Slocum."

"John. Call me John."

"After the *Sea Warrior* was lost, I found myself indigent. I stayed with friends for a while, but . . . but soon decided that I should find gainful employment." Florabelle stiffened even more, as if resolve returned to her small body. Slocum guessed she didn't stand much taller than five foot one or two and couldn't have weighed a hundred pounds dripping wet. But her small, finely formed body contained a man-sized portion of courage.

"You're going to work for Mrs. Winchester as her personal secretary?" he hazarded.

Florabelle shook her head sadly. "Although I have the education—I was fortunate enough to attend the finest finishing school in Boston—that position was not open with Mrs. Winchester."

"Is that why you weren't traveling with your family? You were back East?" asked Slocum.

"My finishing school graduation occurred after the *Sea Warrior* was to sail. My father deemed it best for me to complete the full course of my studies, then take the railroad across the continent while they went around Cape Horn. We . . . we were to meet in San Francisco and begin a new life. My father was an engineer."

"If he was a railroad engineer, why'd he go around the Cape?" asked Slocum. "It might be cheaper for freight, but he and your family could have ridden the rail lines on an employee pass."

"He was not a locomotive engineer," Florabelle said. "He designed them. He was to work with Mr. A. J. Stevens."

Slocum shook his head. The name meant nothing to him.

"Mr. Stevens is the master mechanic who built El Gobernador, the most powerful engine ever designed," Florabelle said, as proud as if she'd done the work herself. "And Papa was to work with him."

Florabelle dabbed at the tears that formed once more. "This is the first time I've brought myself to speak of it, Mr. Slocum. You must think me a complete fool."

"Not at all, Florabelle. Your father sounds like he was a smart man, one to be proud of."

"He was," the brunette said in a low, distant voice. "And all I am able to do is work as a maid."

"How'd you come by this job?"

"Through the headmistress at my school. She and Mrs. Winchester were close friends. When my family was lost, I had no one else to contact. I thought Mrs. Murchison might help."

"Mrs. Murchison was your headmistress?"

Florabelle nodded. "She said that since I was already in San Francisco she would contact Mrs. Winchester, that there was no reason for me to make the trip back to Boston. She was very nice to me. As nice as the situation warranted."

"So she got you the maid's job?"

Again the quick, almost curt nod. "Things have worked out well. I spoke with Mrs. Winchester's secretary while she visited in San Francisco and, because of Mrs. Murchison's recommendation, I was given the job. She arranged for me to drive this buckboard down to the Winchester mansion, saving me the cost of a stage."

Slocum looked over at Florabelle. "You don't even have the price of coach fare?"

"John," she said, "I have only a few dollars left. The rest I had spent on rail fare and expenses. To begin this job, I would have walked, had it been necessary."

Again, she impressed Slocum with her determination. Fate hadn't been kind to Florabelle Jackson, but she wasn't buckling under.

"Think there might be a job of some kind for me at the Winchester house?" he asked. "I've got even less in my pocket than you do. The road agent took almost five hundred dollars, all in greenbacks. Don't have spit left."

"John!" she said, again shocked at the brutality of the West.

"I'll get it back—and more," he said, determination of his own returning. He flicked the reins a bit harder and the mare glared at him. San Jose was an hour down the road, the Winchester mansion another fifteen minutes' easy driving.

4

"That's it?" Slocum asked, disappointed. He had expected a rich widow to live in a huge home. He couldn't even see over the top of the hedge. "Doesn't look like much, though keeping that hedge trimmed must be a full-time chore."

Slocum reined in the swayback mare and stopped in the center of the rutted road to stare at the two-story hedge surrounding the Winchester house. Slocum tried to figure out what the strange-looking trees were which were poking their tops up inside the compound.

"Those are palm trees. Mrs. Winchester favors tropical plants highly," Florabelle Jackson explained. Seeing Slocum's skeptical look, the lovely brunette said primly, "I have seen pictures of them. I know."

"Amazing what education does for you," Slocum said.

He'd hoped that he might be able to get a job with Mrs. Winchester until he had earned enough to buy a horse and get on with hunting down the road agent who had bush- whacked him. He wasn't going to let that son of a bitch get away with it. Slocum knew he might never see the money and there wasn't any way in hell he could bring back to life a good roan horse lying dead alongside the road, but he could keep the road agent from plying his trade on others.

Slocum made a considerable effort to pull his hand away from his Colt. He had fingered the gun as he thought of what he was going to do to the bandit.

"What's that noise?" he asked. He tipped his head to one side and listened hard.

"Sounds like carpenters at work. Are you any good with a hammer, John?" asked Florabelle.

"Done my share of carpentry in my day," answered Slo- cum. "Reckon I can get work?"

"It is my understanding that Mrs. Winchester desper- ately needs all the carpenters she can get. There is a great deal of work being done around the house."

Slocum shook his head. From the road there wasn't any sign of a house even existing. The hedge ran a goodly distance, then vanished at right angles. It might enclose ten acres if it ran as far as Slocum thought it did. Why go to all the trouble of growing such a big hedge? he wondered. The estate stood far enough outside San Jose to insure privacy, if that was what the woman wanted. The tall, well- groomed hedge looked like needless work.

"There's the front gate," said Florabelle. The brunette looked apprehensive. "John, let me go inquire. They . . . they may not take kindly to you being with me."

"I know I look like something the cat dragged in," Slo- cum said. "No argument about that. But that's no reason to get riled. If anything, you helping me out like you did should count even more in their minds that they hired the right one for the job."

"It's only a maid's position," said Florabelle. "Mrs. Winchester has peculiar ideas of propriety. She wouldn't like me showing up with a strange man."

"I'm no stranger than most in these parts," Slocum said. This brought a small, shy smile from Florabelle. She came as close as he'd seen her to actually laughing.

"John, you look *much* stranger than most, especially any who'd work for Mrs. Winchester. You truly do need a bath and a shave."

"Go see about your job. If they don't want me getting inside their fancy hedge, that's all right. I can go into San Jose and find a job there. This entire area seems prosperous enough to support a man willing to give an honest day's work for an honest day's wage."

"Don't you go running off now, John," said Florabelle, stepping down from the buckboard. She straightened the wrinkles in her light brown gingham dress as best she could, pulled herself up to her full five-foot-one height, and walked briskly to the heavy wooden gate mounted in the hedge. Florabelle lifted the ornately wrought, massive brass knocker and dropped it three times. The loud echoes momentarily drowned out the sound of hammers at work.

Slocum bided his time, leaning back in the buckboard seat and trying to find a comfortable position. In less than a minute, the gate swung open a fraction. Slocum saw a man inside—from his looks he might be an Oriental—who played as secretive as the mistress of this estate. Florabelle and the man talked for several minutes. Slocum couldn't hear the words but he got the gist of the conversation.

He heaved a sigh and straightened in the seat. It looked as if he might be carrying his gear back into San Jose. The Oriental had no desire to let Slocum within the gates.

Florabelle stamped her tiny foot and raised a cloud of dust. Her voice lifted so Slocum heard it distinctly. "You will so let him in. He is in distress."

That seemed to have no power over the Oriental, but Slocum heard Florabelle end with, ". . . he is a carpenter." This opened the gate wide.

Florabelle motioned for Slocum to drive inside. He did so slowly, reaching over to help her up. The Oriental—a gardener, from the look of his clothing and the equipment hung at his broad leather belt—glared at Slocum and Florabelle. Slocum politely tipped his dusty, battered hat, then drove along the immaculately kept roadway toward the house.

Slocum revised his opinion. This was no mere house. It was truly a mansion. He let out a long, low whistle between his teeth. There must be at least forty rooms in this incredible structure. Scaffolding was up and carpenters were working to put on another.

Slocum reined in for a moment, looking at what they did.

"Is anything wrong, John?" asked Florabelle.

"Look real careful at where those men are working. Do you see anything wrong?"

"Wrong? Why, no, I don't think so."

"They're finishing a doorway that'll open into empty air," said Slocum. "There's no stairway under the door. See?"

"Well, yes, now that you mention it. Perhaps they'll put the stairs on later."

"Damn fool way to do it," Slocum opined. "Best way is to build the stairs up to the door, then finish framing it. This way, you might have someone inside the room open the door and take a two-story fall to the ground."

Slocum looked closely at the way the house was put

together. His amazement grew. Windows had been boarded over on the inside and through one half-open door he saw a blank wall. The door opened onto a solid brick wall!

"They've a mighty real need for someone who can read blueprints," said Slocum. "Unless they want to make mistakes like that. Getting a job here might drive me plumb loco."

"Surely, some less skilled worker has made a grave mistake," said Florabelle, but her weak voice carried no conviction. More loudly, she said, "There's Miss Merriam. She's Mrs. Winchester's secretary. And niece, too, I believe."

Slocum saw a dour, middle-aged woman with a look of severe disapproval on her face. She had dark hair with gray streaks pulled back in a bun that made her look ten years older than she was. Miss Merriam, although she dressed richly enough in a fine wine-colored brocade dress and patent leather shoes shined so bright that they looked like dark beacons in the sun, did nothing much to enhance her looks.

"Miss Jackson," the secretary said with barely restrained anger, "nothing was said of you bringing a *man* with you. Mrs. Winchester will *not* approve, mark my words."

"Please, Miss Merriam. This is John Slocum. He was set upon out on the road by a robber. His money was stolen and his horse shot out from under him."

"Mrs. Winchester does not tolerate vagrants. We will not feed him. He must leave immediately."

"He knows carpentry," said Florabelle, almost defensively. Her wide brown eyes flashed to Slocum, as if trying to apologize for this rudeness on Miss Merriam's part.

"Is that why Mr. Yamaguchi allowed him inside the estate?" Miss Merriam eyed Slocum with open skepticism. "Wait here one moment," she said. She vanished up a flight of mahogany steps and through a door with some of the finest wood carving and beveled glass work Slocum had ever seen. She returned with a roll of blueprints. She thrust them at him, saying, "Read these for me."

Slocum unrolled them and studied the plans for a moment. "Don't know exactly what you want me to say. There's some strange things here. This wall should go on for another two feet to match up right with the rest of the room. And here—see this set of doorways? Four in one wall less than a foot apart, all leading into the same hallway. And that's not even the strangest part. This stairway leads straight up to the roof, but there's no provision made for a door at the top. You'd walk up those stairs and bang your head."

"That's enough," Miss Merriam cut in. "Obviously you can read blueprints. Can you use a hammer? A saw?"

"Better'n I can read blueprints," said Slocum.

"You'll have to work with others. Right now we have twenty carpenters and assistants on the grounds. You must learn to take instructions and carry them out to the smallest detail."

"Like putting in a stairway that ends flush with a solid ceiling?"

"That is only a part of it. You must never question Mrs. Winchester's motives or requests. I am Margaret Merriam, her niece and secretary. I hire and I fire. There is no recourse to any decision I might make, however you might dislike it."

"No appeal to Mrs. Winchester?" asked Slocum.

"Mrs. Winchester never, and I stress *never*, sees any of the hired help, except for myself and Mr. Yamaguchi."

Slocum read a bit more into what Miss Merriam said. He figured that none of the hired help ever saw Sara Winchester, either.

"We pay well, Mr. . . . ?"

"Slocum, ma'am. John Slocum."

"We pay well, Mr. Slocum. Two dollars a day, plus room and board. If you agree to the rather strict terms of employment, you will bunk with the other unmarried men."

"Two dollars a day is right fine pay, Miss Merriam."

"You will begin on the midnight to eight in the morning shift."

"You work at night?"

"We work twenty-four hours a day." Margaret Merriam's tone warned him not to ask why. "As we have done for the four years Mrs. Winchester has owned this house."

"I've got nothing against working all night long, ma'am," said Slocum. Mentally, he tallied up the money he might earn from such lucrative pay. Fourteen dollars a week was a princely sum for a carpenter, even one keeping odd hours. A month at this job, no matter how loco it looked putting on rooms that had doors opening into thin air and stairs that went nowhere, and Slocum could move on.

"Mr. Yamaguchi will show you to the bunkhouse and introduce you to the others. Pay heed to everything he says. It is essential that you learn the schedule of all that happens on the estate and abide by it. Your role is vital."

Slocum nodded. He felt more like an actor accepting a part in a stage play than a carpenter, but if Miss Merriam —or Sarah Winchester—was willing to pay this well for his services, he could tolerate a tad of eccentricity.

Slocum went to get his gear out of the back of the buckboard. He heard Miss Merriam begin chiding Florabelle again for bringing a strange man along with her—even a skilled carpenter traveling alone with a single lady was not really proper. Mrs. Winchester's niece then launched off into a long list of Florabelle's duties and responsibilities. The young woman trailed behind the secretary, obediently nodding and making polite noises. Just before she vanished through the finely wrought door, the brunette turned and smiled at Slocum.

He saw and returned it.

"You," came the sharp command from the gardener. "You come this way. Drive buckboard to back of house. Don't crush daisies! They are Mrs. Winchester's favorite."

All the way around the house, Yamaguchi lectured Slocum on how to avoid damaging any of the plants so carefully tended on the grounds. Slocum had to admit that the Japanese gardener had done a fine job of tending the grounds. They looked more like something out of a fancy oil painting than a real garden.

"I just noticed the path in," said Slocum. "Lined with palm trees, Miss Jackson said." He peered up at the towering date palms. "Why didn't you match them up, one across from the other? This way there's thirteen of them. Isn't that a mite unlucky?"

"Ask no questions," snapped Yamaguchi. "Mrs. Winchester values number thirteen most highly. It brings luck for her, she says. Everything in house has thirteen of this and that. Here, there, all with the number thirteen." Yamaguchi shook his head, a sad expression telling Slocum that the Japanese did not approve of his employer's tastes in this mystical matter. "Even bathtub drains have thirteen holes."

Slocum had to laugh at this. Yamaguchi turned swiftly. "You do not laugh. Ever. This is condition of employment. No one mocks Mrs. Winchester."

"Not mocking, but it does seem . . . different."

"Hmm, yes, different. It is good that you understand this." Yamaguchi crossed his arms and sat silently as Slocum pulled the buckboard up beside a well-kept barn. They got down, Yamaguchi pointing out where Slocum could store his gear. Everywhere, even in the barn, Slocum noticed the number thirteen cropping up. The inside walls were finished, as if this were the sitting room of some fine lady.

"Do the horses appreciate all this decoration?" asked Slocum. He went to one wall of a nearby stall and ran his fingers over the carving. He had no idea what it was supposed to represent, but the carved beast had a horse's body with a long, slender horn poking from its nose. "Real fine work. Better'n anything I can do. Hope you're not expecting me to do any carving."

"You hammer, you build. That's all. Come along."

Slocum followed Yamaguchi down a well-tended path with a rainbow of blooming flowers on either side. Less than a hundred yards farther along the path rose a two-story building.

"Barracks. Find a bunk. You will begin work at midnight. Your shift boss will tell you what to do." With that, the gardener stepped over the border of flowers and knelt beside a catalpa tree, tenderly pulling brown leaves from its limbs. Slocum entered the barracks. The insides were more like he'd have figured. Unlike the barn, these were plain, painted walls. Everything was clean and serviceable. He looked around until he found a top bunk that wasn't obviously staked out.

Slocum heaved his bedroll up and onto it. He froze when a slight noise behind him alerted him that he was no longer alone in the room. He heard someone enter the long, narrow bunkroom, but before he could turn the sound of the hammer of a pistol clicking into place echoed like a thunderclap.

"Don't even think about reaching for your gun," came the cold command. "There's nothing I'd like better'n to blow you to hell and gone, even if I'd have to clean up the mess that'd make."

Hands at shoulder level, Slocum slowly turned to see a man holding an ancient Colt Dragoon in a rock-steady hand.

5

"I hope your finger's not getting too tired," Slocum said. His eyes fixed firmly on the gun in the man's hand. The finger wrapped around the trigger had turned white with pressure. Slocum judged how much more it would take before the old Colt Dragoon sent a chunk of lead in his direction.

It wouldn't take much, he decided.

"Don't even think of going for your gun," the man said. "Who are you?"

"The new carpenter," Slocum said. "Miss Merriam just hired me on not a half-hour ago."

The man holding the gun scowled. Slocum didn't look like any carpenter, not with the well-worn gunbelt and the Colt that had seen heavy—and probably expert—use.

Nothing about Slocum's attitude bespoke a carpenter, either.

"Name's Slocum."

The man with the pistol spat, accurately hitting a polished brass spittoon in the corner. "Mrs. Winchester don't cotton to men dippin' or smokin'," he said. "But she knows better'n to keep us from doin' it outright."

"Thanks for the warning," Slocum said.

"You really are workin' here?" the man demanded.

Slocum nodded. The tension slowly faded from the man's trigger finger. With ease he released the hammer and put it back down gentle-like. Only then did Slocum relax.

"You always greet newcomers that way?" he asked.

"Been some strange things happenin' around here. Can't be too careful."

"Strange things, meaning road agents?" asked Slocum, interested in both the man's answer and his reaction to the question. The man didn't show any noticeable concern about this problem.

"Don't care spit for road agents. Let the sheriff handle 'em," said the man. "I mean strange things here on the grounds. Damned if I don't halfway believe the old woman's right."

"Mrs. Winchester?" asked Slocum. "What is it she believes? Other than knowing how to pay a man for his work."

"Name's Benny Buchanan," the man said. He looked over his shoulder, as if someone might be spying on him. "Can't be too careful 'round here. Mrs. Winchester has ears everywhere. Damn gardener's the worst. Yamaguchi reports everything back to her like one of those damn parrots the sailors carry 'round on their arms."

Slocum mentally filed the information about the gardener for future use. If he wanted anything to reach Mrs.

Winchester's ears, Yamaguchi would be a good way to do it.

"But you're right about that, Slocum. She does know how to pay a decent wage. Can't find a better job anywhere in the Bay Area, from here up to Frisco."

"What about Mrs. Winchester?" Slocum pressed. "You said she was right about what she believed."

"Oh, that," said Buchanan, hardly paying attention now. The man shook his head and dropped to a bunk. He lay back, hands laced behind his head. "She's crazy as a loon, mark my words. Thinks there are Injun ghosts roamin' about the place."

"Ghosts?"

"*Injun* ghosts," Buchanan corrected. "The ghosts of all those killed with her husband's rifle. Some damnfool medium back in Boston put that bug in her ear. Mrs. Winchester struck to it like a cutthroat trout going after cheese bait."

"As rich as she is, you'd think she'd worry more about being robbed. She has some valuable items sitting out in plain sight." Slocum couldn't keep his mind off the road agent who had robbed him.

"Has six heavy vaults around, they say," said Buchanan. "Wouldn't know about that, but it's probably true. But what robber's fool enough to break into *this* house? It'd take a month just finding a door that led somewhere useful."

"The insides are like the outside?" asked Slocum.

"Doors that don't lead nowhere, stairs with more'n forty steps that don't rise three feet total but have a dozen switchbacks in 'em. Any robber'd go crazy tryin' to escape, if'n he's lucky enough to even find one vault."

"I saw some blueprints that Miss Merriam had. Then they weren't just a test. They were actually used to build the room," Slocum said, more to himself than to Buchanan. This struck him as incredible. The old woman had gone off the deep end, believing the ghosts of Indians killed using her husband's invention stalked her.

"You catch on real quick," said Buchanan, seeing understanding light up Slocum's face. "The ghosts get into the main house and end up all confused and dizzy. Everyone knows dizzy, confused ghosts can't hurt nobody."

"Reckon that's so," Slocum allowed.

"Sound of hammerin' keeps 'em at bay, too. That's why Mrs. Winchester has us work night and day. As long as we're adding to—or takin' away from—the house, the ghosts don't like it none and keep their distance."

"Taking away? You mean we put up rooms, then tear them down?"

"Sometimes. Sometimes the room gets all built around and becomes as permanent as anything can in this Bedlam."

Slocum tried to picture what one of those crackbrain-designed rooms would be like on the inside. A dozen doors, or maybe just one. None? Windows that looked square into blank walls, stairs that went nowhere or maybe switched back on themselves a dozen times just to get up or down a few feet.

Sara Winchester had to be crazy, he decided. Then he laughed.

"What's so funny?" asked Buchanan.

"I was thinking Mrs. Winchester was crazy, but she can't be. If she's got as much money as I think, she's got to be eccentric, instead."

"That's a good one. Poor folk are crazy, rich folk turn eccentric." Buchanan lifted himself up on his elbows and stared straight at Slocum. "I'm likin' you more and more, Slocum. You're gonna make this place come alive. As it is, nobody's havin' any fun."

"Why's that?"

"Strict rules," Buchanan said. "Mrs. Winchester gave in on dippin' snuff but there's no changin' her mind about takin' a snort of corn now 'n' then."

"No liquor at all?" asked Slocum. Just thinking about whiskey made him hanker for a shot or two. Knowing that it wasn't allowed within the confines of the high hedge made him even thirstier.

"None at all. And that's not the worst of it. The married men live with their wives and families a couple hundred yards farther from the house. We ain't allowed no female visitors at any time. Man can get real horny knowin' that he's to be denied liquor and women."

"Reckon so."

"Even worse," went on Buchanan, "it's a long ways into town. We get one day out of the week free. Hard to make it into town and back before we got to be workin' again."

"The money's good, though," said Slocum.

"Like workin' in a prison at times, but you're right."

Slocum looked at Buchanan for a moment. Then he asked, "Does everyone go around armed? You surprised me, coming in with your gun drawn. I wasn't expecting to meet up with anyone this quick, either."

"Sorry about that. The butler, he has me ridin' the hedge to sort of keep things calm. This business about the Injun ghosts has got some of them in the big house spooked. The butler figured that havin' a patrol wasn't such a bad idea. I get an extra five dollars a week for ridin' around and seein' if I kin see anything."

"Have you seen anything?"

"Not a damn thing. But some of the boys claim to have seen a ghost."

Slocum wasn't sure if Buchanan believed in Indian spirits or not. From the sound of the man's voice, he was just happy to be able to carry his ancient Colt.

"Much trouble otherwise?" asked Slocum.

"None. They keep a tight rein on us all. The first sign of trouble and you're tossed out. Sometimes they got men lined up for damn near a mile tryin' to get hired on here."

"I was lucky, then."

"Musta been," said Buchanan. He yawned mightily, stretched, then sank back. The man's eyes slowly closed and in a few minutes he was snoring loudly. Since no one had come by to tell Slocum anything different, he decided to follow Buchanan's lead. Slocum jumped up into the bunk he'd chosen and rested his head on his bedroll. In seconds he, too, slept the sleep of the righteous.

Slocum came instantly awake at the sound of heavy boots. A dozen men, sweaty from work, came in and flopped on their bunks. Less than a minute later, a tall, well-built man came in, planted his feet, and bellowed, "Supper in ten. Get your asses over to the kitchen right now! And be damn sure to wash up before you set down to eat. Mrs. Winchester was complaining to all hell and gone about the filthy lot of you swine at supper last night."

"Aw, Hormel," grumbled one man, "what's the old bat know? She's never set eye on a one of us."

"Cut the talk and be there." Hormel scanned the rest, then his gaze fixed on Slocum. His dark eyes narrowed and his lips thinned to a line.

"Who the hell are you?" he demanded.

Slocum introduced himself, saying, "Miss Merriam hired me on. Mr. Yamaguchi said to find a bunk."

"You a carpenter? You don't look like one." The man studied Slocum like Hormel wanted to see what was running inside, boring and probing. Slocum's cold green eyes never flinched.

"Doesn't much matter what I look like. I can use a hammer."

"You won't be needing that." Hormel pointed to Slocum's gun. "We don't allow hands to go around armed. Mrs. Winchester doesn't like it. Says that's what caused all her problems."

"I heard," said Slocum. "Shame about all those Indians killed by her husband's rifle."

Slocum thought Hormel would explode. A dark cloud of anger formed, but, struggling, the man held back his wrath. "Get over to the kitchen for supper. Follow these idiots. Most of them have it straight where to eat by now."

With that, Hormel spun and left the room. Slocum watched him go, wondering where he'd seen the tall man before. Something familiar about Hormel worried him, but before he could remember Benny Buchanan interrupted his thoughts.

"We go to the second kitchen. The other one's for feedin' the Meskins."

"Mrs. Winchester separates us?"

"Has something to do with her sense of propriety, I heard Miss Merriam say. The Meskins, they get one kitchen to themselves, the Spaniards another, the Orientals still another—and I think we get a fourth one all to ourselves, but I can't swear to that. Come along. They serve according to a rigid schedule."

"Eat on time or don't eat?"

"Those are the rules."

Slocum found the food passable and a sight better than he'd been eating on the trail. He finished and walked out into the small garden area. He shook his head at the marble statues and fancy benches. All this was art, he supposed, but it couldn't hold a candle to the sight of a decent desert sunset, a mare foaling, or the majesty of a herd of buffalo stretching as far as the eye could see.

"Benny," he called. "Miss Merriam said I'd be working from midnight till eight. What am I supposed to do until then?"

"Anything you please. Just don't go wanderin' into the house or stray too far from the grounds. Sometimes it's damn hard to get back through that hedge Yamaguchi tends."

Slocum left the man in the bunkhouse and walked around the grounds. The place reminded him of fancy parks he'd seen in some of the bigger cities. St. Louis had one like this. Jackson Square in New Orleans had statues and fountains, too, but none was as fine as the ones on the Winchester grounds. Slocum felt as if he'd fallen into a dreamworld.

And in the dreamworld, the sound of rooms being built onto the main house never stopped. He wondered how Mrs. Winchester didn't go crazy—crazier, he amended—due to the constant hammering. He could see why it would drive off ghosts. It would drive off just about anyone who wasn't deaf as a post.

Slocum found a quiet spot and sat on a marble bench. If he was only given one day a week off, that would make tracking down the road agent a mite harder. But first Slocum would have to earn enough money on this job to buy a horse. He heaved a deep sigh as he watched the sun setting over the high hedge. It was getting on to seven o'clock, and he would have to be on the job in another few hours.

A rustling sound in the bushes behind him made him stiffen. When the sound came again, he rose, spun, and went into a crouch, his Colt out, cocked, and aimed.

"Come on out real slowlike," he said. "If I see any sign of a gun, you're dead."

"Please, John," came a familiar voice. "I didn't mean to frighten you."

Florabelle Jackson emerged. Slocum released the hammer and let it down, then returned the sixshooter to his holster.

"Sorry," he said. "Reckon I'm still on the restless side."

"I shouldn't have been creeping through the garden like some renegade Indian," said Florabelle. "But my first day at work has made me think differently."

"Making you into a raving lunatic, too?" asked Slocum, with a laugh.

"Something like that. You can't believe what it's like with her. Mrs. Winchester, I mean."

"You've seen her?"

"No, she sees no one except Miss Merriam and Mr. Yamaguchi. And possibly the Chinese butler, but I haven't met him yet, so I cannot say. But I'm sure she's seen me."

"How's that?" Slocum watched the gathering dusk cast faint shadows across Florabelle's beautiful face. He might have seen a more desirable woman in his day, but Slocum couldn't rightly remember. Nor did he want to. Simply watching Florabelle and savoring her loveliness was enough for the moment.

"She has spy holes put in most all the rooms in the house," Florabelle said indignantly. "She actually *watches* us!" The young woman was clearly shocked.

"Maybe she's afraid you'll steal the silver."

"A prudent woman might have some fears on that score," said Florabelle, "but what are we supposed to steal in the—" Slocum thought she blushed—"bathroom? Mrs. Winchester watches us while we attend to our toilet!"

"How do you mean, watches?" Slocum thought Florabelle's embarrassment heightened her delicate beauty, adding distinct color to her pale cheeks. It was almost more than he could do to keep from taking her in his arms and kissing her.

"Just that. The doors to the bathroom are made of clear glass, and I've seen the spy holes she's cut into the walls. It frightens me, never knowing if Mrs. Winchester is watching or not."

"Think she's watching us now?" asked Slocum, moving closer to Florabelle.

"I doubt it. At sunset she's busy with preparations to ward off the nocturnal ghosts." Florabelle stopped talking and lowered her head, as if studying the way her fingers wove intricate patterns in her lap. "I'm not supposed to be out here, you realize," she said.

Slocum put his finger under her chin and lifted. Florabelle's lips parted slightly in invitation. He accepted.

Their lips met, brushed lightly, then crushed together as their passion mounted. Florabelle's arms encircled Slocum and squeezed with more force than he'd have given her credit for. He pulled her close and felt the firmness of her breasts through the fabric of her blouse.

She finally broke off the passionate kiss and tossed her head back, her soft brown hair floating out on the cool breeze gusting through the garden.

"If any of the staff finds us, John, we'll both be fired. Mrs. Winchester does not approve of such licentious behavior between unmarried employees."

"Do you approve of such licentious behavior?" he asked.

Her answer came in the form of another kiss, even more passionate than the first. Florabelle's lips moved apart enough to allow her pink, darting tongue to tease Slocum's. He felt himself responding fully to the brunette now. Florabelle had seemed so prim and proper, but he recognized the devils of lust becoming unchained within her.

Again she broke off. "This Greek marble isn't the best place for us," she said.

Slocum yelped as Florabelle held onto him and simply fell backward, carrying him with her. They landed in a soft pile of leaves behind the bench.

"This is *much* better," Florabelle declared. Slocum had to admit that it was. Lying side by side let him move his fingers along the line of her jaw, across her moist lips, to her closed eyelids. He felt the flutter there as she sighed. Those fingers worked lower, again across her lips to the swanlike throat and still lower. He began unfastening her crisply starched white blouse.

But it wasn't quick enough for the woman. "Here, let me help," she said. Nimble fingers worked and soon Florabelle lay half naked beside him, her small, firm breasts looking like marble in the light of the rising moon. But no marble had ever been so warm and yielding.

Slocum kissed first one breast, then the other, running his tongue up and down the tender slopes. Florabelle moaned softly and thrust her chest up for more attention. Slocum couldn't deny her. He took one hard, coppery tip in his lips and began sucking. Gently at first, then harder and harder as Florabelle begged for more.

"Please, John, oh, yes, yes, John!" The woman's fingers found the buttons on his shirt and opened them. He shrugged out of his shirt while she unfastened his gunbelt and let it drop under the bench.

Slocum began shifting position and Florabelle accommodated him. Hiking up her skirt, she managed to expose even more intimate territory. His hips rocked forward and the tip of his rigid manhood brushed across a moistness that excited him even more.

"Do it, John. Don't stop now. Don't tease me. I need you so! I need you moving inside me!"

Where had the prim, proper schoolgirl gone? Slocum didn't care. He liked this wanton, eager woman much more. He slid forward a few inches. Soft folds of feminine flesh closed around him. Florabelle stiffened and wiggled down to take even more of his hard length into her body.

He rocked back, then levered himself forward, burying himself fully within the heat and moisture of her young, tightly clinging body.

"Don't want to crush you," he mumbled. The sensations flooding his body made it hard for him to talk. He could barely keep from pulling back and slamming into her body. But she was so tiny, so fragile. He didn't want to injure her.

"You fill me so. Oh, John. Don't worry about *hurting* me. You're pleasuring me!"

He leaned forward, his hairy chest brushing across the brunette's turgid nipples. Every movement made Florabelle gasp and moan that much more in pleasure. When she lifted her legs and locked her ankles around his waist, Slocum knew he was trapped. There was no escaping the pleasure they gave to one another. He began rocking to and fro, slowly at first, then with greater speed and desire.

The moonlight cast its pale light on their intimately struggling bodies and turned them into quicksilver sculptures. Slocum looked down into Florabelle's eyes and saw a reflection of his own ardor. His smooth, rhythmic hip movements began to turn ragged as the lust built within him.

But he didn't want to let go till he was sure Florabelle had all she could take. When she gasped, thrust upward, her arms around his neck and pulling him down forcefully, he knew she wouldn't have any complaints. He moved faster and faster, the friction of their mutual lust setting fire to his loins. Slocum couldn't hold back any longer.

He cried out when he felt her all around his rigid, throbbing length. Florabelle might seem inexperienced, but no virgin had ever learned how to hang onto a man like she did to Slocum.

Spent, exhausted and sweaty from the lovemaking, he sank down, his chest pressing against hers. Florabelle smiled and kissed him. Slocum rolled to one side as the woman's legs released their lock around his waist.

"I've never had a man that good, John," she said.

"Miss Jackson, ma'am, I certainly misjudged you." Slocum kissed her on the end of her pert, upturned nose. "You learned more in that finishing school than how to read Plato."

Florabelle giggled like a young girl as she snuggled closer in the circle of his strong arm. "You flatter me, sir. There were many things Mrs. Murchison didn't know about her students' education."

"I'm glad."

They lay with their arms around each other for some time, exchanging soft kisses, stroking over each other's cooling body.

A sudden sound made Slocum sit bolt upright. "What's that?" he demanded.

"I . . . I don't know. It sounds like a fire bell!"

They dressed hastily. Slocum didn't want to see Mrs. Winchester's fabulous mansion burned to the ground—not before he'd put in a single day's work.

6

John Slocum got his shirt buttoned and strapped on his gunbelt just as Florabelle was sitting up.

"Get dressed. But stay back. If this pile of lumber is on fire, it'll take everything with it."

"John, wait!" Florabelle called. But Slocum was already loping along the garden path. His eyes scanned the dark mass of the mansion for signs of fire. No tongue of flame appeared through a window, but then some of these windows might open only onto a blank wall. Slocum didn't know and cursed his ignorance.

The bell rang again.

Slocum ran hard and rounded the corner of the mansion, to come to a complete stop, gasping and out of breath. All around, men stretched and yawned and moved slowly toward a toolshed. No one seemed upset over the ringing bell.

"What's going on?" he asked, seeing Benny Buchanan.

Buchanan yawned widely. "Wondered where you'd got to, Slocum. Time to go to work. The butler rings the bell at midnight to let us know the shift's starting." He yawned again. "But don't pay no nevermind when he rings the damn bell at two in the morning. That's to tell the ghosts it's time to go home."

"Shaddup, Buchanan," grumbled another carpenter. The man took a broad tool belt from those in the tool shed and strapped it around his waist. "You know that Mrs. Winchester don't much like you talking about her beliefs."

"Fact is," said Buchanan, unconcerned at this criticism, "the butler's not ringin' the damn bell to let us know to start. He's ringin' the damn bell to attract ghosts."

"What?" Slocum wasn't sure he understood a word of this.

"Fact is, ghosts don't carry timepieces, so the butler's got to let 'em know when to come."

"I thought Mrs. Winchester wanted to keep them out." Slocum found a tool belt and strapped it on. He didn't like the idea of putting his holstered Colt into the tool shed, but he didn't have time to return to the bunkhouse and stow it properly.

"Only the bad Injun ghosts. She wants to attract the good ghosts, whoever they are." Buchanan shrugged and shook his head sadly. "It's like you said earlier, Slocum, she's as crazy as . . ." Buchanan's voice trailed off. He bent over and busied himself with filling the pouch on his belt with tenpenny nails.

Slocum looked up and saw a dark figure on a balcony. Even as he watched, the cloaked figure with the veil slipped into deeper shadow. He remembered what Florabelle had said about Mrs. Winchester spying on her household help. She might not draw the line there. She might want to see what her carpenters did.

"You, Slocum," came a grating voice. Hormel stalked up, the look of perpetual anger etched on every line of his weatherbeaten face. "I want you working with Buchanan tonight until you prove you're worth your salt. Expect me to check up on you during the shift."

"You the supervisor?' asked Slocum.

Hormel glared at him, turned, and left without answering.

"Don't get him riled none, Slocum," warned Buchanan. "Hormel's a mean one. Think it's because of his first name."

"What's that?"

"Clarence. Hormel hates it. Won't let nobody call him anything but Hormel—or Mr. Hormel, if he's feelin' especially mean."

"Get to work, you layabouts!" shouted Hormel.

"See?" Buchanan winked, then pointed the way for Slocum. Slocum followed along a path that led to the north end of the house. Two others were already hard at work, hammering away at a frame for a wall to be lifted into place.

"What're we doin' tonight?' asked Buchanan.

"New wall. Goes in front of the old one."

"Without tearing down the standing wall? That doesn't—" Slocum bit back the words. He'd started to say it didn't make any sense, but what did make sense about this crazy house? If Sarah Winchester wanted to pay them to put up double walls, double walls would go up, and that'd be that.

"Have at it, Slocum," urged Buchanan. The man started lining up two-by-fours and getting them nailed into a frame. Slocum started at the other end. It had been a few years since he'd had much call to do any building, but the skills came back to him quickly enough. Buchanan was only a stud or two ahead by the time they met in mid-frame.

"Up we go," said Buchanan. Together, he and Slocum lifted the heavy wall while two others secured it at the corners, their flying hammers making quick work of it.

"Do we finish wallboarding it or do we go on?" asked Slocum.

"We go on," said Buchanan. "Another crew will finish this off. Tomorrow, next week, never—who the hell knows?"

Whistling as he went, Buchanan climbed a flight of steps to one side and stopped at the top to call down to Slocum. "What're you waitin' for? It's a good hour till the butler calls in the ghosts with his bell."

Buchanan went inside, Slocum close behind. For a moment, Slocum wasn't sure they even ought to be in this room. The luxuriously furnished room looked like something a railroad magnate would build for his own pleasure.

The four-poster bed was hung with delicate lace curtains. The peach-colored silk bedspread looked inviting enough to lie down on, but Slocum refrained. The rug under his worn boots carried intricate patterns. He knelt and ran his hand over the fine weave.

"Comes from one of them furrin places," said Buchanan. "Persia, I think I heard tell."

"This room is worth a fortune!" Slocum exclaimed.

"And we're supposed to help it along. See over yonder? The linen closet?"

"That's bigger'n any two bedrooms I ever saw," said Slocum. He had thought he was over being surprised at the grandeur and opulence of the Winchester mansion, but he wasn't. "Are we supposed to tend to the maple ward-robes?"

"Look at 'em closer," invited Buchanan.

Slocum approached hesitantly, expecting trapdoors to open under him or the walls to move unexpectedly. Everything he had seen about this loco house made him wary.

But what he found when he examined the maple cabinets more carefully made him shake his head. "These aren't maple. It's redwood painted to look like maple grain."

"You do know your wood," said Buchanan with some admiration. "I worked on the damn things for well nigh a week before I twigged to that. Mrs. Winchester's got some weird ideas, but this one has merit. Maple's harder'n shit to work with. The redwood's more convenient and we can get it by the mile if we like."

Slocum studied the job. Half the wardrobes were completed. The other half needed finishing. He glanced back into the sumptuous bedroom, then took another look at the linen closet. The family farm back in Georgia had hardly been larger than this closet.

"Let's get to work," he said.

"One wardrobe a night's all we're supposed to do. We got other duties."

Slocum set to finishing the redwood cabinet. Just as he rocked back on his heels to take a look at his handiwork, he heard a bell tolling mournfully.

"Don't let it worry you none," said Buchanan. "That's the warning for the ghosts to skeedaddle."

"So they'll know to get home in time," said Slocum. He couldn't understand why anyone went to all this trouble over a ghost, good or bad. All he believed in was what he could touch, see, hear, taste, shoot.

"That butler carries the best damn chronometer in the

entire Santa Clara Valley. Maybe in all California. Heard tell that Mrs. Winchester paid five hundred dollars for it. Can't let them ghosts get off schedule." Buchanan snorted and finished off the cabinet. He stood and wiped his hands on a rag.

"What now?"

"Our last job for the night'll be in one of the screwy rooms upstairs. If'n I can remember how to get there."

Slocum followed, memorizing the path. They made several cutbacks that seemed to have no purpose, but Slocum said nothing. However he did it, Buchanan led them to an upper-floor room with thirteen windows and seven doors. Slocum said nothing about the oddness of the room's shape. No two of the walls came together in a right angle. The subtle difference made him a little giddy. It was almost a pleasure to look out the windows and down into the garden.

"Benny," he called. "What's that? Down in the garden?"

The burly man sauntered over and peered over the window sill. "Don't see nothin' worth mention. What did you think it was?"

"Something white moved by that tower."

"That's the bell tower. The butler reaches it through some kind of secret underground tunnel. Nobody but him and Mrs. Winchester knows how to get to it that way. They don't want just any yahoo ringin' the bell and maybe confusin' the ghosts, I reckon."

Slocum continued studying the garden below. Again there came a flash of white. Slocum levered open the window with some difficulty; the frame had been warped slightly to accommodate the bulge designed into the wall.

"What you fixin' to do, Slocum?"

"Someone's down there. I mean to find out who. Didn't the butler hire you to ride guard during the day, since there's been odd things happening here?"

"That he did, and when I go ridin' out, I have a gun. That old Dragoon ain't much of a gun, but it's a damn sight better'n nothing at all. Which is what we got right now."

"Whoever's down there just went into the kitchen."

"Wait." Buchanan grabbed Slocum's shoulder and kept him from sliding out onto the sloping roof and dropping into the garden. "There's a quicker way to see what's goin' on."

Slocum hesitated, then made his decision. Benny Buchanan knew his way around this house better than he did. He would bow to the man's superior knowledge.

Buchanan left by one of the seven doors, stopped, frowned, returned to the room, and shrugged, then chose another door. This led along the roof to a greenhouse. He pointed to one of the thirteen windows.

"There. Just below the window. Look there and see if there's anything worth mentionin'."

Slocum found a tiny window of curious design. At first he thought it was beveled glass such as decorated so many of the doors. Then he saw that it was a magnifying glass.

"I'm looking straight down into the kitchen!" he exclaimed.

"It's one of Mrs. Winchester's spy holes. Don't rightly understand how this one works, but it has mirrors and a magnifying glass in it. Some of the other ones look into the women servants' bedrooms." Buchanan cleared his throat and smiled. Slocum didn't ask him how he'd come to know of them.

Slocum pressed his eye close to the glass and stared down into the main kitchen. Drifting through the shadows came a white flash. Slocum caught his breath. The image shimmered and danced in the looking glass.

"A ghost!" Slocum gasped. He moved around to get a

better look. The ghost passed close enough to whatever device Sarah Winchester had hidden in the kitchen so that Slocum saw jagged dark lines drawn across the flat white face: Indian war paint. On the naked white chest Slocum saw a herringbone of reds and blacks, more war paint, but from what tribe Slocum couldn't rightly say.

"No shit," said Buchanan. "Lemme have a look-see." Buchanan pressed close and peered over Slocum's shoulder. Slocum relinquished his spot and let the other man stare at the apparition.

"That's the damnedest thing I ever seen," declared Buchanan. "Looks to be headin' toward the dining room. Let's see if we can't meet that son of a bitch face to face."

"You're not afraid of a ghost?" asked Slocum.

"There's too many things in this world I am feared of," said Buchanan, "that I don't have time to be 'fraid of no ghost." Buchanan chuckled. "Never saw nothin' that couldn't be explained some way."

Slocum had to approve of the man's attitude. He'd come across too many otherwise reasonable men who turned paler than the "ghost" downstairs at the mere mention of burial grounds. During the War, he had had occasion to cross more than one battlefield still filled with the bodies of soldiers from both sides who had fallen in combat. Slocum had heard weird wailings and moanings and seen glows that he couldn't explain, but not once did he figure he was watching a ghost. It might have been wind or St. Elmo's fire or even swamp gas taking on a spring glow, but he was sure that once a Minie ball went through your gut, you died. There was no lingering in this world waiting to get to another.

Slocum believed in God and Heaven and Hell. What he didn't believe in was getting caught halfway between this world and the next.

"There. Down those stairs," said Slocum.

"Wait, lemme think." Buchanan stopped and scratched his stubbly chin. "Might work. Don't remember all this part of the house. We might be gettin' near Miss Merriam's bedroom. Wouldn't want to disturb her none. She gets riled easy enough, as is."

Slocum took the steps five at a time. The risers were hardly an inch high but the stairs wound back and forth. These had to be ghost-trap stairs that Mrs. Winchester insisted on. Slocum had to admit that it did a good enough job slowing human travel.

He swung around the bottom of the stairs and looked out over a confusing array of doors. A considerable amount of construction was in progress along this corridor, most of the material just stacked to form an obstacle-laden path.

"Jeee-zus!" exclaimed Buchanan. "Think I may be changin' my mind."

Slocum turned and saw that Buchanan was staring into a dining room to their right. In the room stood the Indian ghost, quick hands filling a burlap sack with silverware taken from a large, ornately carved cherrywood cabinet.

"He's stealing the silver!"

Slocum leaped over a pile of lumber, rocked against the doorjamb, and burst into the room. The ghost looked up, startled. Slocum stared into kohl-darkened eyes that seemed bottomless. The war paint and the dead white were all Slocum could focus on. The Indian ghost let out a war whoop and vanished.

"Where'd he go?" Slocum asked, stunned.

"There're secret passages all over this damned house," said Buchanan. "Maybe he knows of one over there."

Slocum and Buchanan went to the cabinet. The drawers had been jerked open and now stood empty, the evidence that valuable silver had been stolen. Slocum ran his hands over the edge of the cabinet looking for a latch that might let the cabinet swing away from the wall and reveal a passage. He found nothing.

Slocum dropped to his hands and knees and looked at the floor. Faint footprints remained on the inlaid wood floor to indicate the recent passage of a barefoot man. Even as he looked at the floor, the indistinct outlines vanished. No trace of the ghost remained.

"Where does this hall lead?" asked Slocum. The only possible escape route for the ghost lay along a narrow corridor winding into the bowels of the Winchester mansion.

"Can't rightly say," said Buchanan. He rubbed his fingers over the edge of the opened silverware drawer. He wiped his hand on his shirt and shook his head. "We better get our asses out of here or we'll be accused of stealin' the family treasures."

"But we—"

"You don't understand, Slocum," Buchanan cut in. "The way Mrs. Winchester has built this house makes her damn sure that none of the evil spirits can get inside to bedevil her. Since only good ghosts are called and can roam around as they please, that means one of the hired help has to have light fingers.

"Look around," Buchanan went on. "You don't see no ghosts. Who do you see who's likely to catch all the blame? One of them's named Benny Buchanan. The other's John Slocum."

Slocum started to argue, then fell silent. Buchanan knew more about the workings of the Winchester household than he did. What the man said made sense: Accuse those on the scene. Who, even a lunatic, would believe the story that the silver had been taken by a ghost? Better the men in hand than the ghost flitting through the house.

Slocum wanted to look around the room and examine it

more carefully for ghostly spoor, but he knew Buchanan spoke the truth.

"How do we get back to the greenhouse?" he asked.

Buchanan smiled weakly and shook his head. "Don't know, but we'd better find a way soon. I don't want Hormel coming along to check up on your work and not be able to find us."

Slocum started into the labyrinth, finding it more difficult backtracking than he'd thought. He agreed with Buchanan. Getting Hormel mad on the first night of work wasn't smart.

Slocum just hoped that he wouldn't get permanently lost in the maze of rooms and stairs.

7

John Slocum's entire body ached from the work. He flopped onto his bunk alongside the others on his carpentry shift, but unlike the others, he didn't fall asleep immediately. He lay staring up at the bare, whitewashed ceiling of the bunkhouse, his mind turning over and over all he had seen that night.

"The ghost," he murmured. "What was it? *Who* was it?" He had no illusions that it had truly been an Indian's ghost. What use did a dead Indian have for expensive silverware? If a real Indian had been intent on thievery, he'd have gone directly for the barn to steal the horses. The mansion's liquor supply might have been raided, too. But silverware? Slocum saw no reason. To an Indian, there was no honor in stealing the white man's eating utensils.

Slocum yawned and rolled onto his side. Was there even a liquor supply? Mrs. Winchester had banned whiskey in the bunkhouse. Did this apply to those in the main house, too?

Slocum groaned softly when he rolled onto his belly. His back still ached from the blows the San Francisco crimp had landed, but more than this, his arms and shoulders hurt like hell from the night's exertion. Mrs. Winchester had got a full day's—night's—work out of him. He had worked on the false wall, stained redwood to look like maple, then reframed all the windows in the seven-door, thirteen-window room. But, more than this, he'd seen the Indian ghost raiding the house of the Winchester valuables.

Indian ghost.

Those words ran over and over in his head until he finally fell asleep.

The ringing bell brought Slocum instantly awake. For a moment, he thought he'd slept the entire day through and it was the midnight summoning of the good spirits. He blinked as a ray of bright sunlight fell across his face. It couldn't be later than noon. When Clarence Hormel came into the room and began bellowing, Slocum sat up.

"What's wrong?" he managed to ask. There were many others asking the same question.

"Mrs. Winchester wants all hired hands to assemble in the garden immediately!" Hormel shouted. "You have five minutes. And try to look respectable. She doesn't like it when you show up with chin stubble and uncombed hair."

"What is this, the army?" muttered one man. Hormel went to him and loomed over the bunk, glaring down.

"Any more lip out of you, Morgan, and I'll see that you're walking back to town without a job."

"Come off your high horse, Hormel," Morgan said, sit-

ting up and running his fingers through his greasy hair.
"I'm moving. Just give me a minute to wake up."

"Five minutes," Hormel said. His hard eyes locked on
Slocum's. A thrill of danger ran through Slocum, but he
didn't understand why. Hormel didn't have anything
against him. They didn't even know one another, and as far
as he'd been able to tell, Hormel's inspection of his work
the night before had been superficial, as if the man really
didn't care if Slocum was a good carpenter or not.

Something deeper ran through the dislike, Slocum
guessed. Had he met Hormel before? Was that why the
man seemed familiar, and why he seemed to carry a grudge
against Slocum? Slocum tried to remember all the men
he'd faced across green felt card tables in San Francisco as
he accumulated his stake. Hormel might have been one,
but Slocum didn't remember any single big loser in the two
months he had played there. The sailor on the last night at
Irish Mike's was the only hardcase, and that had come
more from being drunk than from feeling cheated.

Maybe it was just Hormel's way. Slocum dropped to the
floor and pulled on his trousers. He needed a few more
hours of sleep, but if Mrs. Winchester called, they had to
go.

Buchanan rubbed the sleep from his eyes as they went
to the garden. Benny said, "Stay in the back of the crowd
so's the butler can't see you. The chink gets nasty mean if
you show up to one of these sessions looking like yesterday's shit."

"What do you think they want?" Slocum eyed Buchanan.

The burly man straightened slightly. "We can both haz-
ard a pretty damn good guess about that, I reckon."

Slocum followed Buchanan's suggestion and stayed
well back, positioning a marble deer squirting water from

its mouth to form a fountain between him and the balcony where everyone's attention was fixed. Two figures dressed in black emerged and came forward.

For a moment, Slocum thought Mrs. Winchester was going to speak. But the woman on the balcony was Miss Merriam, and the man had to be the Chinese butler. The butler stood with thick arms crossed, his face all ice and storm. Slocum knew that this wasn't going to be a pleasant get-together.

"I am severely disappointed," said Margaret Merriam. "Mrs. Winchester has given you all fair, decent salaries, living quarters superior to anything else you'll find in the Santa Clara Valley, and how do you repay her generosity? *You steal from her.*"

The words rang like the clapper of a bell inside Slocum's head. Miss Merriam wasn't above dismissing the lot of them if it pleased Sarah Winchester.

"Mr. Yamaguchi and I have had several of you on patrol through the grounds during different shifts. These men claim that no one from outside has sneaked onto the estate grounds. We believe them, having stayed up many nights ourselves to watch."

"Seems they want to believe it's one of us," said Buchanan in a low voice. "Hell, the days I rode guard, damn near anybody could've snuck past me. There's six acres enclosed by those hedges. That's a lot of space for someone willin' to hide out."

Slocum nodded. He wondered about the highwayman who had robbed him. Would he view the Winchester mansion as a plum ripe for the picking? Hearing stories about the six vaults hidden away and filled to overflowing with real treasure might be enough to entice any ambitious robber.

"We are therefore imposing a curfew and restricting

everyone to their quarters when they are not working," went on Miss Merriam. "We do not like to take such action, but Mrs. Winchester feels it is necessary to stop the pilfering."

"What was taken?" called out one man.

"An expensive set of silver was stolen last night," Miss Merriam answered. The woman's mouth set into a grim, determined line. "The thief was not seen."

"Then how do you know it was one of us?" called the same man. "You're makin' us out to be crooks when we're just concerned with doin' our jobs."

A murmur of agreement went through the crowd.

"Any of you who cannot abide by the new regulations are free to leave. Mrs. Winchester has authorized a generous severance allowance of two weeks' wages."

"Damned attractive," said Buchanan. "But I got nowhere else to go. Reckon I'll be stayin' on, ghost or no ghost."

"Should we tell Miss Merriam about what we saw?" asked Slocum.

"You can. I value the job a mite more'n you seem to. Even them ghost-fearin' folks wouldn't believe what we saw."

Slocum had to agree.

"You are all dismissed. Return to your duties or the bunkhouse."

The crowd began to break apart. Slocum looked back over his shoulder and saw the butler motioning to Clarence Hormel. The foreman talked briefly with the butler, the thunder clouds of anger building like a violent summer storm. But the foreman only nodded agreement and stalked off.

"Slocum, Buchanan," came Hormel's sharp voice. "Hold it. They want to see you." Hormel looked toward the now vacant balcony. *"She* wants to speak to you."

"Who's that?" asked Slocum.

"Mrs. Winchester. Get on over to the main sitting room. Move, damn your eyes!"

Buchanan and Slocum exchanged glances. It was deucedly hard for Hormel to take this, they saw. Slocum figured that not many people ever had a personal audience with Mrs. Winchester and that this unexpected attention didn't sit well with Hormel.

Slocum couldn't say he was any too pleased about it, either.

Slocum rubbed his hand across his stubbled chin and decided that there wasn't time to shave properly and get gussied up to meet his employer. The way Hormel spoke, those awaiting him were impatient.

He and Buchanan went into the kitchen, found a stairway leading up, took a wrong turn, and opened a door that dead-ended into a brick wall. They backtracked, then found an airshaft. Slocum called up to a maid, "How do we find the sitting room?"

The woman jumped as if Slocum had stuck her with a pin. For an instant she fussed about as if she hadn't heard. Then, almost as if talking to such lowlifes as Slocum and Buchanan was a sin, she pointed toward the side of the house.

"Thanks, ma'am," said Slocum, but the maid didn't acknowledge.

"What're those things?" asked Buchanan, stopping to stare at a rack filled with small funnels, dark red rubber hoses attached to their spigots and vanishing into the wall.

"Speaking tubes," Slocum said. "Riverboat pilots use a similar contraption to signal their engineers when they want more speed or to reverse engines."

"Mrs. Winchester must have them all over to contact

her house servants. Never out of touch with her staff. A nice way of keepin' things runnin' real smooth-like," Buchanan observed.

Slocum remembered what Florabelle had said about the clear glass in the bathroom doors. More likely, Mrs. Winchester just refused to let anyone get away with anything, and this provided her the means to command anywhere in the house from some central location.

Slocum smiled at the thought. A central command post. A spot where everything throughout the house might be seen. The fancy spy mirror system in the third-floor greenhouse that looked down into the kitchen might be only a hint of what Mrs. Winchester had built into this massive pile of lumber.

They found a spiral staircase that spun up three stories. "Reckon this is what the maid was pointin' at?" asked Buchanan.

"Might as well try it."

Slocum started up, stumbling occasionally on the oddly spaced risers. When he came to the second floor, he had to step over a doorway almost ten inches high. At the end of the hallway stood Miss Merriam, arms crossed and a look of severe displeasure on her face.

"This way." She pointed into a room to her right. "Don't keep Mrs. Winchester waiting one instant longer."

"No, ma'am," said Slocum as politely as he could. His heart picked up speed as he neared the room. He would finally get to meet Sarah Winchester face to face. A week ago that prospect would have meant nothing to him, but the mystery surrounding the woman had turned this moment into something special.

It didn't happen the way Slocum had thought it would.

He and Buchanan entered a large sitting room. As with the other occupied rooms in the mansion, this one was appointed lavishly with brocaded loveseats, rugs that cost more than Slocum had earned in his life, delicately carved Portuguese cork tiling on the walls and ceiling, and furniture constructed by the finest woodworkers in the world. All that was missing was Sarah Winchester.

"You, Mr. Slocum. Mr. Buchanan," came a voice from an alcove across the room.

"Yes, ma'am?" answered Slocum, straining. He started to cross the room, but the Chinese butler interposed himself and slowly shook his head. Slocum stayed his ground but didn't try advancing.

The voice came from behind a wooden screen with patterns of ducks and marshes carved into it. "You know what happened last night during your work period, do you not?"

"Miss Merriam told us."

"My niece thinks it was one of you men. *We* know better, do we not?"

"You saw something that makes you think different than Miss Merriam?" asked Buchanan.

"*We* saw him!" shouted Mrs. Winchester. "We saw the Indian ghost take the silverware. We know it was a messenger from the spirit world come to haunt me!"

Slocum and Buchanan exchanged looks, then Slocum tried to figure out what the butler thought of all this. His impassive face betrayed no hint of emotion. Slocum decided he must have heard all this before and remained unmoved. Behind them, Margaret Merriam stirred uneasily.

"Aunt Sarah—" she began.

"Be quiet, Margaret. These men saw the specter. It was one of the evil spirits I was warned about. My cleverest traps have proven ineffective. This ghost managed to enter in spite of the sound of hammering—or was there a moment when no one was at work? Mr. Slocum?"

"Well, ma'am, that might happen, just for a minute or

two. Construction doesn't always mean hammering. There's a goodly amount of sawing and shaping, too."

"See?" Mrs. Winchester cried, vindicated. "It *is* possible that the ghost spirit entered and avoided all my traps. I must not be as safe as I thought."

"This entire house is one giant trap, ma'am," said Buchanan. Slocum knew he was baiting Mrs. Winchester. Even worse, so did the butler, who glowered at Buchanan.

"But not good enough, not good enough by half! If you see this Indian scalawag again, let me know immediately. I cannot tolerate him roaming unchecked through my home."

Slocum started to speak, but the butler put one finger to his lips, signaling Slocum to silence. The Chinaman herded Buchanan and Slocum from the room and back to the hallway where Miss Merriam stood.

"My aunt spent last night awake and pacing nervously in her bedroom. She saw something she thought was a ghost. I will not have her upset further over this matter. Neither of you will mention this to the other workers. And neither of you will have anything to do with any so-called Indian spirit."

"We didn't want to—" Slocum began. Miss Merriam cut him off with a gesture.

Slocum and Buchanan began retracing their footsteps and got lost in the maze of corridors. They finally blundered out a side door and had to circle the entire mansion to reach the bunkhouse.

"The old lady thinks there really is a ghost," said Buchanan. "What about you, Slocum?"

John Slocum shook his head. People believed what they wanted to. If Sarah Winchester wanted a denizen from the spirit world, she would be inclined to see one. All Slocum had seen was a sneak thief.

8

"You look like you're gettin' ready to go huntin'," said Benny Buchanan. The man lounged back on his bunk and peered at Slocum through a half-opened eye.

John Slocum closed the loaded cylinder of his Colt and checked to be sure that he had an adequate number of extra rounds of ammunition in both gunbelt and vest pocket. He'd worked for fourteen solid days without any time off. Now Hormel had given him three days to do with as he pleased.

Slocum was going hunting for the road agent who had robbed him.

"Snipe," said Slocum. "I'm hunting snipe."

Buchanan laughed. "You can't fool me none, Slocum. You're goin' into San Jose and do some cattin' around.

Find yourself a good whorehouse and spend the entire three days there."

"Whatever you say, Benny."

Slocum had accumulated enough money to buy himself a plug horse from one of the other carpenters, a married man who needed the money for his sick wife more than he needed a horse that threatened to eat him out of his pitiful savings.

"Bring back a snipe or two for me. Always loved eatin' 'em. 'Specially the purty red-haired ones." Buchanan laughed again, then rolled over. He had told Slocum that he intended to spend his entire time off sleeping. The days he hadn't been working as a carpenter, he'd been riding the perimeter of the Winchester estate to make sure that no human got in or out without permission.

Of the Indian ghost they hadn't seen a trace after that first night, although Miss Merriam had reported seeing it drifting through an upper-story hallway less than a week back.

The secretary had remained close-mouthed about it, but Slocum heard from Florabelle Jackson of more thefts attributed to the ghostly visitor—and that Sarah Winchester was beside herself with worry over how the evil spirit had managed to sneak past all her carefully contrived spirit traps with such ease.

Slocum wished he'd been just a tad faster getting into the dining room that first night, or that the "ghost" had been slower in escaping. Slocum had the gut feeling that the highwayman and the ghost were tied in together. Why he thought that he couldn't rightly say. Something, though, worked deep down inside his mind, and he always trusted his instincts. They'd kept him alive for a goodly span of years.

Slocum rode out the front gate, Mr. Yamaguchi noisily

slamming the heavy wooden portals behind him. From the gardener's sour expression, Slocum wondered if the Japanese ever wanted to see him come back. Nothing had gone right for Yamaguchi. The daisies that were Mrs. Winchester's favorites had been dying, the boxwood trees were losing their small, round leaves, and someone had been cutting away at portions of the huge hedge surrounding the estate.

Slocum rode slowly because he had to. The decrepit mare couldn't go much faster than a walk, but Slocum was in no hurry. He still ached all over from the hard work, but he didn't mind that too much. Hard work never hurt anyone, he thought. But the work!

So much of it was pointless. He'd built cupboards that had no shelves, doors that hinged on the wrong sides, doors scarcely three feet high, items he couldn't even put a name to. Work was good, but he preferred to see useful results after he'd finished.

But the pay had been good, he couldn't deny that. Mrs. Winchester paid promptly every Friday morning at eleven o'clock. For that steady flow of good, hard gold eagles and double eagles he would keep on for a while longer. Or until he found the man responsible for trying to drygulch him out on the road.

The need for revenge burned brightly in Slocum. All that a man had in the world was his honor. He felt that his honor had been besmirched by the road agent. That he'd been robbed of a considerable sum of money was inconsequential. Slocum figured never again to see even a plugged nickel of his San Francisco earnings, but he *would* see the robber brought to justice.

Slocum touched the handle of his Colt. If he couldn't find a sheriff who would take care of the highwayman, he'd bring a bit of justice to the Santa Clara Valley himself.

Slocum rode along, enjoying the spring weather, trying to keep his mind on the problem facing him. Cold-tracking the crafty robber was going to be hard. Almost a month had passed. Whatever spoor he was likely to find would be useless—or worse, it might mislead him. But Slocum knew that road agents liked to stake out a portion of territory and would operate there exclusively until the law got too hot on their trail. This allowed them an important edge; they would know the country better than just about any victim.

By midday he had reached the place where the outlaw had shot the roan from under him. Slocum dropped to the ground and began studying the signs. "Damn little," he muttered to himself. He wiped away a flood of sweat damming up under the brim of his Stetson, then led his horse toward the spot where the shootout had occurred.

A bright, shiny cartridge casing caught his eye. He picked it up. "From a Winchester," he said. "Which means nothing. Everyone carries a Winchester, or just about." Although it had been B. Tyler Henry and his patents that had made the Winchester rifle as good as it was, it had been Oliver Winchester who had marketed the weapon and made sure everyone knew of its excellence. Slocum dropped down to a sitting position, bouncing the casing in his hand. And it had been Oliver's son William who had married Sarah.

"Such a chain of events," Slocum said. The swayback mare shifted her weight, turned, and peered at him from a large, watery eye, as if asking why he even cared. "And it all ends with Sarah Winchester, a woman who's crazy as a loon."

Slocum stood and slowly walked along the ridge where the road agent had fired upon him. No hoofmarks remained in the dust. Slocum had expected none after all this time.

He walked and looked, hoping for a hint as to the identity of the bushwhacker.

He was so intent on his task that he jumped when a voice demanded, "Who'n hell are you, mister?"

Slocum's eyes snapped up and found the man doing the talking. His hand stopped halfway to his gun. The man mounted on a dappled gray gelding silently standing under a nearby tree wore a battered tin badge that caught occasional beams of sunlight filtering through the trees.

"Afternoon, Sheriff," Slocum called out, coming out of his crouch to face the lawman. He hoped that the man wouldn't get too riled at the way he'd almost got drawn down on.

"I asked you a question. Who are you? And I'll add another. What you doin' out here? You trailing someone special?"

"Name's Slocum. As to who I'm tracking, I don't know his name, but he ambushed me and robbed me of damn near five hundred dollars about a month ago."

"Didn't get no report on it across my desk," the sheriff said suspiciously.

"Never actually reported it, since I got shot up a mite in the process. Had my horse killed and I was scratched across the shoulders. Been doing some recuperating since then."

The sheriff rode forward and looked over the mare, a sour expression on his face. "You been workin' over at the Winchester place, haven't you? I recognize this nag. Belongs to Willie Joe Nance."

"Mine now. Bought her."

"Whatever you paid, you got rooked. This animal's more dead than alive. She'll die under you before you get fifty miles."

The horse snorted in derision at such a dire forecast.

"Don't need to go that far to find the road agent who robbed me," said Slocum.

"You after the reward?"

Slocum shook his head. He hadn't known there was a reward and said so.

"Posted the fliers on a couple dozen trees hereabouts," said the sheriff. "A hundred dollars for his capture. Not much compared to the money you said you lost."

"And my horse," said Slocum. "The roan was worth close to that. It was a good horse."

"You have any information about this highwayman you maybe should pass along to the law?" asked the sheriff.

"This might be the casing from the rifle he used to shoot me," said Slocum, holding the shiny brass up for the lawman's inspection.

The sheriff spat and looked even more disgusted. "Could've come from anyone's rifle. Hell, I carry a Model '73 myself. So does everybody in these parts. Old Sarah don't like it none, but we all know a good rifle when we see one."

"The outlaw been working this road pretty regular?" asked Slocum.

"Regular enough so's Wells, Fargo and Company is beginning to get annoyed with me. They've lost four shipments over the past six months. And that's not saying nothing about people traveling the road who've been held up."

"The road agent doesn't seem to be greedy," said Slocum. "How many robberies in the past six months can you lay at his doorstep?"

"A dozen or so, not counting the Wells, Fargo shipments. Call it one every two, three weeks. That's more'n enough to keep me patrolling the road and looking for him."

Slocum said nothing. With a record like that, the road agent must live in the Santa Clara Valley and only venture out on rare occasions. A new thought occurred to him. The robber wouldn't have to work the road as often if he could steal from Sarah Winchester's mansion.

"You got the look of a man who's just thought of something important," said the sheriff. "What is it?"

"Nothing, Sheriff."

"Look here, Slocum, I posted that hundred-dollar reward, but I don't have to pay it out if *I* catch the outlaw. You holding back information might not get you that reward as quick as it'll get you time in prison for being an accomplice."

Slocum knew it went deeper than this. The sheriff wouldn't have to pay out the reward if he personally caught the road agent. Even more, that reward would go into his deep pockets. No lawman was paid well. Most of the time they spent serving process for the local judge, maybe getting paid as much as a dollar a summons. Collecting taxes brought in a little more—and some additional graft—but mostly they didn't get much in the way of salary.

Slocum almost laughed when he realized that he was probably getting paid a damn sight more for his carpentry than the sheriff was for keeping the peace.

"The reward doesn't matter that much to me, Sheriff. I'm more interested in stopping him. Nobody kills my horse and robs me and gets away with it. Call it a matter of pride."

"I don't cotton much to vigilantes," warned the sheriff.

"Does it matter how it happens, as long as the road agent is stopped?"

"Course it does. Law's got to be obeyed, otherwise we're no better than the robbers."

"How long you been looking for him?" asked Slocum.

The words had barely left his mouth when the sharp crack of a rifle drowned out any chance for the lawman to reply. The man stood up in his stirrups, made a gasping noise, and then tumbled over backward, falling from his horse and getting his left foot tangled up in the stirrup. The sheriff's gelding reared, then bolted at the unexpected noise and the sudden loss of weight on its back.

Slocum reacted before he even realized he'd moved. He ran four paces, dived, and caught the dangling end of the reins. The horse jerked him around and started dragging him, too, but the weight of Slocum on one rein and the sheriff in the stirrup on the other side brought the horse to an abrupt halt.

Slocum rolled under the horse's heaving belly and freed the lawman's foot. No sooner had he done so than another shot rang out. Slocum heard a click and a bullet's ricochet. The sheriff's horse jumped straight into the air, sunfishing more than any bucking bronc Slocum had ever seen. The bullet had grazed the horse's right front hoof.

Slocum caught the sheriff up under the arms and dragged him away from the fear-crazed horse to keep the man from being trampled. Of his own ancient mare he saw no trace. The animal had apparently ambled off while he was talking with the sheriff.

"What happened?" the dazed lawman asked. "Someone shot at me!"

"That's right," Slocum said grimly. "Your horse is out there bucking its brains out. A second bullet hit it in the hoof. Probably more in pain than you are."

"I'm all right," the sheriff said, sitting up. Just as he did, a third bullet came wending through the trees and smashed into the trunk not six inches above the man's head. The sheriff fell to one side, his hand fumbling for his sixshooter.

"Damnation, no one shoots at me and gets away with it!"

"Any idea who it is?" asked Slocum.

"Don't matter one whit. He's going to be dead meat when I get to him." The sheriff got his pistol out and motioned for Slocum to begin circling to the left. The sheriff would go right and they'd catch the bushwhacker in a crossfire. Or at least that was the plan. Slocum doubted it would work. The unseen sniper had the advantage of surprise and more than enough time to get on his horse and ride like the wind. Finding him if he decided to run would be well nigh impossible.

Slocum scrambled through the small stand of trees, reflecting as he went how familiar this all seemed. He had been ambushed here three weeks earlier. With luck, this would be the last time.

Slocum cocked his Colt as he slid like a lizard wanting to sunbathe across the top of a large granite boulder. His keen eyes surveyed the terrain and to his surprise he caught sight of the sniper.

As before, he didn't get a good look at the man's face. The distance was too great. Slocum cursed, because his handgun wasn't going to fire accurately enough at this range to do much damage. He slid on, slithering down the far side of the rock and running in a crouch. If he could get within fifty feet of the outlaw, that'd be it. One quick aim, the steady trigger pull, and no more road agent.

Slocum got closer and closer as the road agent occupied himself with taking potshots at the sheriff, almost as if he toyed with the man. Slocum didn't care about the outlaw's motives. A few feet more and his career would be over—and Slocum would garner some small revenge for all that had been done to him.

The outlaw stopped firing. He levered a new shell into

the smoking Winchester's chamber, then rolled and stared straight at Slocum, as if he'd known all the time what was going on behind him.

Slocum's eyes widened in surprise. He'd expected to get a good look at the man's face. He didn't. A cloth mask totally covered his features, leaving only nose and eye holes. The cloth had been dipped in something that turned it bone-white.

Shock echoed through Slocum when he realized that what he'd thought to be shadows on the man's cheekbones and other facial features were actually dark lines of Indian war paint. The outlaw wore a mask carrying the same pattern as the Indian ghost Slocum had confronted in the Winchester mansion.

That momentary thrill of recognition froze Slocum. The outlaw rolled onto his back and lifted the rifle. Both Slocum and the road agent fired at the same time.

Slocum's reflexes took over. He jumped to one side, savagely twisting his back as he went. Hot lead took his hat off again, putting still another hole in it. But his hide was intact.

Slocum hit the ground painfully and was almost unable to roll and come to his knees to fire again. Pain from his back injury made him queasy and weak, but Slocum fired. One shot after another he fired directly at the road agent— Indian ghost.

He missed every time. Tears of pain fogged his vision and made his hand shake.

He heard a mocking laugh, then the sound of a horse's hooves pounding on the dry ground. Slocum looked up and through the red haze of pain saw the road agent vanish over a low rise, rifle held high above his head like an Indian brave who has been on a successful raid and is returning to his camp.

John Slocum dropped onto all fours, shook himself like a wet dog, and tried to keep from passing out. All he could say for certain was that he had definitely linked the road agent with Sarah Winchester's ghost—and that he hadn't died doing it. Other than this, Slocum wasn't sure what he had gained.

9

The sharp rock in the center of John Slocum's forehead caused so much pain that it pulled him out of the darkness. He opened his lips to complain and got a mouthful of dust. He choked, spat, and rolled onto his side. The blaze of red-hot pain that shot up and down his spine made him think he'd been gunned down from behind.

But the pain subsided and didn't torment him too much as long as he lay still. Slocum came to realize that he had strained his lower back again when he dodged the road agent's bullet. He was alive, but only the intense pain convinced him of that.

"Couldn't feel this terrible unless I was alive," he said out loud. He reached behind him and rubbed his lower back. The pain again stabbed into him, but this time without the ferocity that it had before. He continued to massage the tormented muscles and finally felt some sensation returning to his legs. He kicked a couple of times, winced at the pain, then sat up. This was almost more than he could bear.

Slocum looked around, trying to find the sheriff. He saw no sign of the lawman.

"Hope he's gone after that son of a bitch bushwhacker," Slocum said aloud, only half meaning it. He wanted the road agent—and Indian ghost—for himself.

Slocum got to his feet and took a few tentative steps. The pain refused to go away, but he managed to keep the urge to simply lie down and die from it corraled. Giving up now would do him no good at all. Slocum put one foot in front of the other and began to walk. After a dozen paces he felt almost human again.

His decrepit old mare looked up from where she dutifully grazed and canted her head to one side, studying him. She whinnied as if saying, "You look worse than I do," then went back to her meal of dry grass and weeds. Slocum didn't mount immediately. He wasn't sure he could make the effort yet.

Instead, he walked around until the pain subsided to a dull, throbbing ache. Slocum started to feel as if he would live, so he cautiously went toward the spot where the road agent had lain in wait. He found four brass casings in the dirt. He took them and examined the butt ends. All four had a peculiar nick, showing that the firing pin had a small cut taken out of it. He dug in his vest pocket and got out the casing he had discovered earlier.

"Same cut spot from the firing pin," Slocum said. He hadn't expected anything different. Heaving a deep sigh, he put the casings into his pocket, patted them into place, and turned his attention toward the stand of trees where he and the sheriff had been ambushed.

Of the sheriff he saw no trace.

"Sheriff!" Slocum called out. "You all right?" No answer. Slocum hurried to the trees and followed the lawman's path. The footprints in the dry dust turned into damp, dark red marks. The sheriff had been hit at least once. And it didn't look like a minor scratch from the amount of blood turning the dust to a bloody muck.

Slocum dropped to one knee when he found the sheriff. The man lay sprawled over a rotting log. Careful not to strain his back any more, Slocum turned the man over. He had seen worse, but he couldn't remember when. The sheriff's chest was soaked from the blood leaking from two close-spaced wounds.

"That bushwhacker's a damn fine marksman." Slocum went cold inside, thinking that he might be up against a sniper of his own caliber. This road agent was at least as good—maybe even better.

The wounded man stirred and his eyes came open painfully. He fought to focus. In a weak voice, he said to Slocum, "Get me into town. Doc can fix me up."

"Save your strength," Slocum said. "It looks bad." He began pulling back the blood-matted shirt. He found the two bullet holes bubbling pinkly. The lead had gone through the lung and every breath the sheriff took caused froth to boil out.

Slocum searched the sheriff's pockets and found a foil pouch of chewing tobacco. He dumped out the crumpled brown weed and smoothed out the foil.

"This isn't going to hurt a bit," he told the injured man. He lied. When he ripped free the cloth around the wound the sheriff passed out. Slocum worked quickly. He doubted the sheriff would live long if he didn't do everything right.

Taking a long strip of the man's shirt, he bound the foil over the sucking chest wounds. The foil would keep the air from outside from entering the chest cavity and collapsing the lung. Other than this, Slocum could do nothing for the man.

The sheriff needed a doctor. Bad.

Slocum got his steady old mare and heaved the sheriff over the back. The wounds might bleed and the man might die this way, but Slocum knew that if he left the lawman alone and went for help, he'd be dead long before anyone could return. Leading the mare, Slocum started off. He saw no trace of the sheriff's horse. The animal had limped away to escape the punishment being given it.

Slocum doubted it had gone far with the bullet-chipped hoof, but he didn't want to take the time to find it. Better to get the wounded man into Los Gatos.

It took over an hour of walking and occasionally burdening the tired mare with both their weights before Slocum arrived in the small, sleepy town. Curious citizens came out onto the board sidewalks to stare at the spectacle presented them.

Slocum called out to the nearest man, "Get the doctor. The sheriff's been hurt bad."

The man stood and stared. Only when Slocum yelled at him again did he move. He took off like shot, vanishing up rickety stairs on the side of the Smiling Cat Saloon. Slocum led his mare to the foot of the stairs. Less than a minute later, a bearded, moth-eaten man came down from the office looking as rickety as the stairs.

"You brought back Sheriff Thompson, eh?" the man said. He shook back long, greasy hair from his eyes and went to the lawman. "Yep, that's the sheriff. Don't look to be in good enough shape to get upstairs to my office. Just drop him over there on the boardwalk. In the shade. No sense cookin' his damnfool brains any more'n needed."

Slocum and two of the men who'd been watching in silence carefully pulled Sheriff Thompson from across the saddle and put him flat on his back for the doctor to examine.

"You did this, eh?" the doctor said, looking up at Slocum.

Slocum nodded.

"Good work. Might have saved the son of a bitch's life. You musta seen wounds like this before, eh?"

"In the War."

"Figured as much. Good thing the sheriff chews, ain't it?" The doctor, for all his poor bedside manner, seemed competent enough. Slocum watched as the doctor probed the wounds, clucking his tongue as he worked. An assistant got the man's black bag and watched in silence with the rest as the doctor did things to the sheriff's wounds and finally began stitching them up.

"That'll hold the bastard," the doctor said at length. "Watch over him, Mitch," he ordered his assistant. "This gentleman's gonna buy me a shot of whiskey for savin' the sheriff's life."

"Why should I buy you a drink?" Slocum asked, more amused than angry at the presumption.

" 'Bout the only pay I'll get is the drink. Sheriff Thompson's not known for payin' his bills promptly—or at all, mostly."

"You patch him up a lot?"

"Not all that much," the doctor said. "But enough. Los Gatos is a peaceful place usually. But Thompson's been gettin' into scrapes lately that put holes in his worthless hide."

Slocum wondered what the doctor's feud with Thompson was all about.

The doctor turned one bloodshot eye toward Slocum, lifted his glass, and saluted. "To our continued good health." The doctor knocked back the shot of cheap whiskey and coughed. His health sounded poor, Slocum thought.

"Is there a deputy?"

"In Los Gatos?" The doctor shook his head. "Next nearest law's over in San Jose, and Thompson don't get along too good with those folks. Feud over serving process a goodly portion of the time. 'Bout the only steady money for a lawman in these parts."

"What's your problem with Thompson?"

The doctor laughed and motioned to the barkeep for another drink. "No trouble what's not family. I married his sister. Lazy woman. Worthless through and through. And Mitch, that layabout who's my assistant. That's Patience's son from her first marriage."

"So everyone who ought to know about this's already been notified," said Slocum.

"Reckon that's so." The doctor coughed again and spat a black gob into the brass spittoon. "You shoot him?"

"Road agent did the shooting. Sheriff Thompson was patrolling out on the road. We got to talking and the road agent took some shots at us. Sheriff got hit."

"And you didn't." The doctor finished off a third shot of whiskey. "That must mean the highwayman wasn't aimin' at you. Damn fine shot, from all that's been said."

"Maybe not," agreed Slocum. He winced in pain as his back acted up on him. The doctor noticed.

"Sore sacroiliac? Got just the thing for it. Ralph!" he bellowed at the barkeep. "Bring me the special bottle. The one you keep hid under the back bar."

The barkeep reluctantly fetched a bottle a quarter full of light brown liquid.

"More whiskey?" asked Slocum. "A good enough prescription, but . . ."

"But nothing. No, don't drink it. Smear it all over your back. Best damn liniment you'll find. Had a bottle of Ralph's special with me when I went to deliver the Dupree baby a while back. Horse pulled up lame. Don't know what made me try this. Soaked a rag in it and wrapped it around the horse's leg. Got better before we reached the Dupree place. Give it a try. If it works on my horse, it'll work on your back. And if'n it don't, go on and drink the swill."

"Thanks."

"Don't thank me till you've tried it. Damn stuff stinks."

"Nothing more I can do here," Slocum observed.

"If you didn't stop the road agent what's been workin' the territory—and neither did Thompson—reckon you don't get any reward." The doctor cocked his head to one side. "'Bout all you can do is buy me one final drink for the road."

"You're not going anywhere," Slocum pointed out.

"But you are, and you're the one what's buyin'."

Slocum couldn't argue with the logic. He bought a final round, then left. Sheriff Thompson still lay on the boardwalk, Mitch tending to him. Slocum saw that there was nothing more he could do—or anyone else, for that matter—so he mounted the tired mare and headed back toward the Winchester mansion.

"Damn foolish on your part, if you ask me," said Benny Buchanan. "You had three days off. Hormel guaranteed them, and you come draggin' back in after only one. What's wrong with you, Slocum? Couldn't find any women in San Jose?"

"Didn't look there," Slocum said.

"Didn't look!" exclaimed Buchanan. "You're out of your mind. Why, you coulda..." His voice trailed off when Clarence Hormel strutted into the bunkhouse.

"Ready for work?" the foreman asked. "Good thing you're available, since Mrs. Winchester fired four of the others."

Slocum didn't ask what the reason was for their sudden termination. Sarah Winchester worked on impulse—or the impulse of her ghostly contacts. Every third night she held a seance somewhere deep inside the house, Florabelle said, and whatever the spirit world told her, she did.

The spirits must have told her to get rid of the carpenters, which left too few to work twenty-four hours a day. Slocum had come back just in time to be cajoled into working another midnight shift until a new crew could be hired in San Francisco.

One thing Slocum had to give Sarah Winchester: She didn't spare any expense when it came to her loco behavior. Hormel had been told to offer five dollars a day, which he did with obvious reluctance.

"We're just getting ready," Slocum told the foreman. He eyed Hormel more intently than he had meant to. The man nervously shifted and almost ran from the bunkhouse.

"Looks as if you spooked him," said Buchanan. "How'd you go and do that? I been tryin' for months to figure a way of chasin' the son of a bitch off and I haven't done it yet. You just look at him and Hormel turns tail and runs."

Slocum said nothing. He, too, had noticed how edgy Hormel seemed in his presence. It was as if Hormel had a guilty conscience. Slocum tried again to remember where he'd seen the man before. It wasn't San Francisco, of that he was sure. But where?

"Let's get to poundin' nails. Nothin' better to do, anyway. Leastways, *you* don't have anything better to do." Buchanan snorted derisively. "Couldn't even find any women in San Jose. Hell and damnation!"

They began work deep within the Winchester house, rebuilding a room so that it had two extra doors that led nowhere. One opened into a brick wall and the other onto a shaft that dropped two stories to the basement without benefit of stairway.

"This is the goldangedest room I ever saw," said Buchanan, hammering the frame of the door into the wall. "Even in this crazy place, it's strange."

Slocum swung out and balanced precariously over the twenty-foot drop as he finished the outside of the door, as ordered. He fumbled slightly and dropped a nail, which went tumbling to the basement. Slocum watched as it went and saw a flash of white on the next level.

"Benny," he said in a low voice. "Get over here."

"Need help, eh, Slocum? Anybody what can't find a woman in..." Buchanan's voice trailed off as he looked past Slocum and down at the first-floor room across the shaft.

"Him again," said Slocum. "And this time I'm not letting him get away. I don't give a damn whether he's man or ghost, he's not getting away!"

Slocum shucked off his tool belt and found handholds inside the shaft. He agilely dropped down a story and swung through the window of the room where he had seen the Indian ghost.

Slocum crouched and hid behind a low divan. He quickly moved behind it until he came to the far end. Peer-

ng around, he saw the ghostly white figure across the
oom rummaging through a small box. The war-paint
narkings on the face matched exactly those of the road
gent who had bushwhacked Sheriff Thompson.

He watched for a few seconds, something stirring at the
ack of his mind. He had seen this man before somewhere
–but where?

Almost as if the ghost heard Slocum's silent thought,
ne apparition straightened and peered around the room.
His dark eyes fixed on the spot where Slocum hid.

Faster than an arrow in flight, the ghost bolted for a
oor. Slocum let out a whoop and went after him.

"Damn!" Slocum shouted as he ran through the door—
nd found an outstretched foot to trip over. He landed face
own, but the air wasn't knocked out of his lungs. He
ecovered cougar-swift and came to his feet, ready for a
ght.

The Indian ghost had fled.

"Where'd he go?" demanded Buchanan, coming
rough the door. The man panted harshly from the exer-
on of getting his burly frame down the narrow shaft.

"Went that way," said Slocum. The two men ran down
e hall. Slocum found it impossible to track easily in the
azy twist of rooms and corridors. He stopped and mo-
oned Buchanan to silence. Listening hard, he heard the
ttling of the house, the distant sound of workmen's ham-
ers—and bare feet running against floorboards. He
rned and got a fix. On feet as silent as any cat's, Slocum
ent stalking. When he opened the door to a room off the
orridor, he caught sight of the white body smeared with
ar paint. He lunged, his hand finding a solid arm. Slocum
abbed and swung the Indian ghost about.

A fist both substantial and human drove for Slocum's
in and missed, glancing off his cheek. Slocum put down

his head and ran forward, arms circling the struggling
body. Behind him he heard Buchanan entering the room.

"Help me with him. He's slippery!" Slocum cried.

The ghost-man twisted and landed a blow that sent Slocum flying. Dazed, he sat up. But the Indian ghost had
once again vanished, gone through one of the seven doors
in the room.

Benny Buchanan vainly looked through one after another. "Don't see him, Slocum. He's gone. I'm beginning
to think the son of a bitch really *is* a ghost. He's too damn
hard to catch."

"He's no ghost," said Slocum. "He's too solid for that."
Slocum looked down and saw a white smear on his pant
leg where the ghost had tripped him. His hands and his
shirt were covered with the same white powder.

He ran a few of the grains of powder between thumb
and forefinger, then tasted it. "Whatever else our visitor
might be, he's not a ghost," said Slocum. "Know what this
is?" He held out a pinch of the powder for Buchanan to
examine.

The other man's face split in a crooked grin.

"Flour," said Slocum. "He covers himself with flour to
look like a ghost, then paints himself up to make us think
he's an Indian."

"One of these nights, we're gonna catch him. Let's pop
him into the oven when we do. He's all ready to bake!"

Slocum sobered. What had the thief been after this
night? He had kept the small box with him when he fled.
Slocum had the feeling that it meant only trouble unless he
acted.

But how?

10

"He was up to no good," said John Slocum. "But what?"

"Stealin', I'd say," said Benny Buchanan. "I thought I saw him carryin' a box. Might have been something valuable he filched in another room." Buchanan turned around and looked through several doors. "I think we're near Miss Merriam's bedroom. She's prone to wear some fancy jewels when she gets gussied up. Don't happen often, but it does." Buchanan let out a long, low whistle of appreciation for the woman's expensive jewelry.

"I think there's a mite more to it than just thieving," Slocum said. The road agent had been active. Why get greedy? And if he was working at the Winchester house, why risk exposure to rob a few more jewels? Slocum thought it would be more logical to find the spots where the Winchester fortune was kept, then steal it in one big robbery.

Why bother with small amounts until the final robbery?

There was more going on than he understood. But Slocum vowed that this would change. He wasn't going to let the Indian ghost get away a third time. He laughed harshly.

"What's so damn funny, Slocum?" demanded Buchanan.

"Twice we tried to stop him and twice we failed. Is the third time the lucky one?" he asked. He looked around at the odd corners of the room, numerology evident everywhere.

"Seeing how this is Sarah Winchester's house," said Buchanan, "we might have to wait till lucky thirteen!"

The two wended their way through the complicated stairwells and down hallways until they found the room where they'd been framing the doors. Working silently, they finished just as Clarence Hormel came in to inspect their work.

"Look all right, Mr. Hormel?" asked Slocum. The foreman only grunted, then turned and left.

"Yes, sir, Mr. Slocum, you do have that man spooked, if you'll pardon the expression," said Buchanan. The burly man wiped his forehead and watched Hormel vanish through a long series of doors. "Now how can I go about duplicatin' your fine effort on that front?"

"There's more things going on around here than I can fathom, Benny."

They finished their shift and started back to the bunkhouse. The sun had been up for several hours and breakfast for the night shift was being served in the kitchen, but neither Slocum nor Buchanan felt like eating. They were drained from their work and the ghost chase and hankered to get sleep before food.

"I'm so tired I could sleep for a month," Buchanan said. "But I promised Yamaguchi I'd go ride around his hedge and make sure no one came in to steal his daisies."

"Doesn't look as either of us will be getting much sleep," observed Slocum. Half a dozen people stood in a tight knot at the door leading into the bunkhouse.

"What's going on?" Buchanan asked one of the men.

Morgan turned and shook his head. "Can't rightly say. Miss Merriam and the butler came bargin' in a few minutes ago and chased us all out. I hardly had time to get my pants on. They're inside with Hormel, tearing the place apart."

Slocum moved so that he could stand on tiptoe and peer through a window. Miss Merriam stood with arms crossed while the Chinese butler and the foreman searched the personal belongings of all the men. A cold thrill of understanding passed through Slocum and settled in his belly. He knew they would find whatever it was the Indian ghost had stolen—and they would probably find it in his bedroll.

"Where you go?" asked Yamaguchi. The gardener stood behind Slocum. The pair of hedge shears in his hand made Slocum step back to keep from getting skewered.

"Nowhere, it looks," said Slocum.

Slocum held his breath when the trio came from inside. Miss Merriam cleared her throat to get everyone's attention. Slocum waited to be singled out as the thief, certain that the ghost must have planted whatever was stolen among his belongings.

"Gentlemen, I am sorry to have been forced to conduct this search, but last night some valuable gems were taken from settings in Mrs. Winchester's jewelry."

When Hormel looked in his direction, Slocum braced himself for the accusation.

"I am happy to report that none of you seem to have been responsible for the theft. Thank you for your patience." Miss Merriam made a quick gesture and the butler silently trailed behind her as if she led him on a chain. Hormel paused for a moment, then hurried after them.

"Now if that don't beat all," said Buchanan. "I told you that they're always lookin' to prove us guilty about something."

"If not us, then who?" Slocum said so softly that no one but Buchanan heard.

"You on the trail of something important?" asked Buchanan. "Like what that ghost's been up to?"

"An idea has occurred to me. If Hormel comes back, alibi for me. Tell him I'm tending my horse."

"Whatever you say, John." Buchanan went into the bunkhouse with the rest of the workmen. Slocum stood for a few seconds trying to decide between following Miss Merriam and seeking out Florabelle.

He followed Miss Merriam, the butler, and Hormel.

Walking quickly, he managed to come parallel with the three so that he was hidden from view by a large marble fountain. The gushing water occasionally robbed him of perfect hearing, but Slocum was able to hear enough to piece together what was being discussed.

"I told you that none of my men were responsible," said Hormel. "It has to be one of the house staff. One of Mrs. Winchester's maids, probably."

"My aunt has perfect confidence in the household staff," Miss Merriam said primly.

"Why does she watch them so?" asked the butler. Slocum didn't hear what Margaret Merriam said, but the butler subsided.

"I simply cannot believe my aunt's story about this Indian spirit roving the house after dark," said Miss Merriam. Slocum heard the slight quavering in the woman's voice. She didn't believe in ghosts, he suspected, but she'd seen the spirit as it haunted the halls of the Winchester mansion. Slocum remembered Florabelle saying that Miss Merriam had seen the spirit with her own eyes and knew it couldn't simply be a figment of her aunt's fevered imagination.

"If there's any thieving going on, it *must* be the maids —or the kitchen help," said Hormel.

Slocum frowned. Why was the foreman so intent on shifting blame to the household workers? Was this the man's way of keeping his own men free from inquiry? Slocum hadn't seen this much loyalty in Hormel, but it might exist. Or—and Slocum couldn't discount this—Hormel might have other motives than helping his men escape suspicion.

"Nothing will be done within the confines of the house without Mrs. Winchester's permission," said Miss Merriam. "And that, Mr. Hormel, is a direct order that will not be violated by you or anyone working for you. Is that clear?"

Slocum had heard orders snapped by the best officers in the army, but seldom had he heard any given with such precision or force. Hormel could never say he didn't know what the woman meant.

"Very well, Miss Merriam. I've got to attend to the day crew. They're beginning a new set of closets in the sitting room on the north side of the house."

"Very well." Miss Merriam and the Chinese butler went into the gloomy house.

Slocum decided not to follow them or Hormel. Instead, he sought out Florabelle Jackson.

Benny Buchanan had been chiding him for not going straight to a San Jose whorehouse on his day off. Slocum smiled now. Why bother with bought women when he had one who was not only willing but who cared for him—and one for whom he cared. Slocum's smiled faded as he considered. Florabelle drifted in and out of his thoughts more and more recently. A woman that handsome made a man think of settling down.

Slocum shook himself free of such a notion. Why would Florabelle want him for a husband? He was a drifter, never content to stay in one place for more than a few months. The wanderlust was too potent—had been since the War. In some places the law still looked for him. Yankee judge killing carried a stench to it that would linger for a lot more years than he had left. And some of the other things he'd got involved in were hardly better. He'd done some bank robbing himself, not to mention a stage or two along the way.

And killing? Slocum had done that, both during the War and after. The judge and his hired gunman were just the start of a string who needed killing.

What could he offer any woman, especially one as fine as Florabelle Jackson? She had been educated in the finest of schools and had only been forced into taking this job with Sarah Winchester because of family tragedy.

Slocum shrugged off this line of thinking. He had learned never to dwell on matters that couldn't be resolved —or that required him to change his own nature.

He didn't know for certain if Florabelle was on duty now. His own work on the night shift made their assignations less frequent than either of them would have liked, and he had trouble keeping up with her schedule. Slocum slipped into the house and walked quietly down a long corridor.

He froze when he heard voices that were all too familiar. He had circled around somehow and come up on a series of windows that opened into Miss Merriam's study. She spoke with the butler and Hormel.

"Mr. Hormel," the woman said, "your concern is noted. However, you will not take any action whatsoever on this matter. I consider it closed."

"But someone's stealing from Mrs. Winchester!" protested the foreman.

The argument went on while Slocum dropped to his hands and knees and ducked under the open windows. He had no good idea what it was they debated, but it probably hadn't changed from before. Hormel wanted to search the household staff's quarters, too, and Miss Merriam rebelled at the idea.

Slocum got past the windows and slipped into Florabelle's bedroom. He waited for a moment, looking all around. Florabelle had told him that Sarah Winchester had a spy hole high up in the ceiling. He finally saw among the ornate curlicue rosewood decorations the tiny glass bead that was her magnifying lens.

He edged around the wall so that he avoided possible observation, should Mrs. Winchester be looking in.

He checked the adjoining room and again marveled at how well even the maids lived in the main house. He had no complaints about the bunkhouse—he'd lived in worse places—but this bordered on the most lavish of hotel rooms he'd ever stayed in.

"Florabelle," he called softly.

The woman was seated in front of a tiny looking glass, patting her hair into place. She jumped a foot when he called her name. One slender hand went to her throat as she cried out and turned.

"Oh, John, it's you. You startled me."

"Sorry," he said. "Didn't want to alert anyone watching."

"I don't think Mrs. Winchester is watching at the moment. She reads her spiritualism books immediately after breakfast. I've never known her to begin spying until early afternoon."

Slocum shook his head. What a way to live. He didn't mind the odd carpentry assignments, nor did he mind living in the bunkhouse, but putting up with such eccentricity was beyond him. He didn't know how Florabelle did it.

"John," she said, in a voice so low he could barely hear, "I don't have to go to work until ten. That's almost an hour."

He looked down at her and felt himself wanting her more and more. The pert upturn of her nose, the waves of brown hair that framed her face like a delicate picture frame, the soft oval of her lovely face. He wanted her; he had to have her. Now.

Florabelle's emotions were running at high tide, too. She swung around on the low stool and stood, her arms flung around his neck. He pulled her up on tiptoe and kissed her lips hard.

"Oh, yes, John. This is the way it should be always. I want you. I do, ever so much!"

He silenced her with his kisses. She threw back her head and let him kiss down the arch of her throat, into the hollow—and lower. He felt her smooth flesh tremble from the light, teasing kisses he gave her now. His tongue pushed aside her bodice and sought the warm flesh of her breasts, but her clothing was too firmly in place for this.

"Here, let me, John. Let me get it loose."

"No," he said. She stared up at him, startled.

"But no one will be spying on us. I don't think Miss Merriam enjoys spying like Mrs. Winchester."

Slocum knew that the secretary was still occupied with Hormel and the butler in her study. Margaret Merriam wasn't likely to be looking in on them, especially if Florabelle wasn't due on duty for another hour. It wasn't this that stopped him.

"Wait. Lean back. Enjoy yourself."

Florabelle didn't relax. She continued to strain on tiptoe, her five-foot frame reaching up to his six-foot one. But Slocum bent over and used his tongue, lips, and teeth to pull first one, then another button free. He jerked back and untied a ribbon fastener, then began burrowing his face down again.

Florabelle sighed with joy. His face was firmly between the gentle mounds of her breasts. He licked and lapped and lightly nipped until neither of them could stand the pressure mounting within them.

"No more, please, no more, John."

"No more?" he teased. "You want me to leave?"

"No!" She was horrified at the idea. "I want *more*, but of this, not your tongue." Her fingers tightened at his crotch, squeezed and made him gasp. It took all his control to keep from acting like a young buck out to get his first woman.

"Let's see what can be arranged," he said. When Florabelle tried to lead him into her bedroom, he resisted. The thought of the spy hole in the ceiling stopped him, even though the four-poster bed had a canopy. Sarah Winchester—or anyone—might happen to look in. He wanted his lovemaking with Florabelle to be private.

"This room's good enough for me." He smiled wickedly. "And I can't wait till you get into bed!"

Florabelle yelped, then laughed with glee when Slocum's knowing fingers dropped down, caught the hem of her skirt, and lifted. Together they worked off her undergarments. Slocum dropped his drawers and let his manhood jerk out into the open.

"No, not that way," Slocum said when Florabelle tried to lie down on the floor. His strong hands lifted her entirely off her feet. He swung her slightly so that she could wrap her legs around his waist. He easily supported her weight. For a brief moment there was a twinge in his strained lower back, but the doctor's liniment had worked well during the night.

Florabelle positioned herself over the tip of his rigid length, then settled down, totally engulfing him with her clutching body. For a moment, Slocum could only stand and shiver. Then he began turning slowly, his hands cupping Florabelle's rear. He lifted and dropped her gently, giving rhythmic in-and-out motion to their coupling. The woman's brown eyes closed and a smile crossed her lips. She arched her back and moaned softly.

Slocum bent forward and teased her exposed nipples, sucked in the firmness of her breast, licked and kissed and lapped. And all the while he was spinning her nipple in a circle.

"Oh, John, this isn't like it's ever been for me," Florabelle sighed. "It . . . it's better! A hundred times better!" She quivered and shook like a leaf in a high wind. When Slocum saw the rosy flush rising to her breasts, shoulders, and neck he knew she was almost ready.

He quickened the movement so that she slid up and down powerfully now. Florabelle began to pant harshly. Her hands around his neck began to dig in. When she tensed all over and crushed herself fervently to his strong body, Slocum could take no more. He felt as if he was a stick of dynamite and Florabelle had lit his fuse.

Slocum exploded with desire, his seed fountaining into Florabelle's eagerly squeezing interior.

Slick with sweat and suddenly weak in the knees, Slocum sank down to the floor. Florabelle relaxed her hold around his waist and stretched out. She purred like a contented kitten, arms extended high over her head, her breasts flattened on her chest. She smiled in the sexiest, most seductive way Slocum had ever seen.

"That was exactly what I needed—wanted," she said. Florabelle reached down and stroked over Slocum's flaccid length. "And I need it again."

"Woman, have mercy!" he cried. "I worked all night. You're going to wear me out."

"I hope I don't wear you down." She rolled up and kissed his limp organ. Suddenly he wasn't so tuckered out.

Denying her was difficult. Then Slocum decided that there wasn't any reason to do a crazy thing like that. He was tired, but not tired enough to turn away a woman like Florabelle Jackson. He bent down and kissed her lips. In a short while, they were again wrestling passionately.

11

John Slocum didn't want to see Florabelle leave, but she had to report for work. He waited in her bedroom for a short while, then decided that no one would be watching for his exit. Bone-tired, he made his way to the kitchen and ate a hearty lunch before returning to the bunkhouse for a well-deserved rest. He slept through the day to awaken shortly after sunset. None of the others had stayed; all had more important things to do with their free time than to spend it in bed—alone.

Slocum stretched and yawned mightily. Then he smiled. Even more than the others, he had something better to do than while away his time alone. Florabelle would be finishing her work and they might pick up where they had left off.

Slocum sobered when he thought of the previous night's encounter with the Indian ghost. Whatever the robber had been up to, it still hadn't come to full light. Slocum wasn't overly eager to find out what devilment would be caused, either. If he had been in the road agent's bloody boots, he knew he'd have to stop what might become a disaster. It would never do having people poking around asking too many questions.

Prevention was a far better way of fighting the ghostly road agent than simply waiting for him to act first. Slocum's shoulders still hurt from the bullet crease, and he remembered Sheriff Thompson's near-fatal wounds.

Still, he felt warm and comfortable and hardly wanted to stir. The idea that he had to stop the Indian ghost soon began gnawing away at Slocum, though, and he finally bestirred himself and dropped to the bunkhouse floor. He winced at the pain in his back caused by the impact, then smiled.

"I'm not in such bad shape," he told himself. Slocum washed up in the delicately painted Japanese porcelain basin at the end of the long room and felt a world better.

Almost good enough to tackle a real ghost.

He thought about supper, then pushed the matter from his mind. Better to meet Florabelle again. Lovely Florabelle.

Slocum stopped dead in his tracks, an idea forming that he'd as soon not consider. If the ghost-robber hadn't planted the jewels he'd taken the night before as a frame-up, what was the point in risking so much to steal them in the first place? Slocum had no doubt they were valuable, but he figured that bigger fish to fry awaited this road agent.

"Florabelle," he muttered. Slocum set off at a pace that wasn't quite a run. He avoided Miss Merriam and the Chinese butler as they tended to small household matters outside the kitchen door, ducked into a hall, and burst into the brunette's bedroom.

Florabelle looked up, startled. "Do you always explode into a lady's boudoir like that, John? Sometimes I find such impudence on your part quite rude."

"Sorry," he said. "Didn't mean to startle you. But an idea came to me that you might be in need of help."

"And how is that?" Florabelle's icy tone told Slocum he would have to come up with a good reason. He hoped that it was a good one.

"Think on it a while," he replied. "The ghost is after something big. My guess is that it's something in one of the six vaults—maybe the contents of all six."

"We have established that," Florabelle said primly. He wondered if she had been in this household too long and had been influenced by Miss Merriam. The tone was nearly identical.

"He can't like the way I've been nosing around. He'll want to stop me for fear I'll put a bullet between his thieving eyes." Slocum quieted down a mite. His words had a sharp edge to them that he hadn't really intended, but the image of Sheriff Thompson and his wounds came back in that instant, and his own twinges reminded him all too well of the misery this man had already caused.

"And?" Florabelle said, her face softening as she understood what this meant to him.

"And he might know about you. I mean about us. There's no good way he can kill me. He's tried enough times and I'm on the lookout for him. But if he tries to get at me through you . . ." Slocum's words trailed off.

"Would that work?" Florabelle asked.

"What? Of course it would!"

The brunette smiled now. "A lady likes to be told she's

important now and again," she said. "You just don't do it often enough. I do so hate to go fishing for compliments like that."

Slocum touched her cheek. The warm flesh aroused him, but he needed to do so much before he could allow himself this pleasure.

"If you keep fishing, you're likely to land one whale of a lot of compliments."

"Now *that's* what I want to hear!" Florabelle rose, stood on tiptoe, and kissed him.

"First," he said, backing off a bit, "we've got to do some hunting. The ghost might be close to getting into the vaults."

"Let Mrs. Winchester worry about her old jewels and money. I know what's really important." The woman tried to show him, but Slocum adamantly resisted.

"Oh, all right," she pouted.

"You know where the vaults are?"

"I know where one is. I happened on it by accident while making up Mrs. Winchester's third bedroom."

"Third bedroom?"

"She never sleeps in the same room two nights in a row. Claims that the spirits might find her if she lingered overlong." Florabelle shrugged. "I have heard stranger things."

"But not recently," Slocum finished for her. "Where is this vault?" A new possibility opened itself to him. What if the Indian ghost had no real fear of Slocum, but considered Slocum impotent to stop him? And what if Florabelle held the whip hand that might stop the thieving—and didn't know it?

"Have you seen anyone around the vault? Looking it over, as if he wanted to break in?"

"John," Florabelle said in exasperation, "I'm not a guard here. In fact, I'm not even supposed to know the whereabouts of the vault. It was purest chance that revealed it to me."

Slocum nodded. Together the pair of them slipped into the corridor. He motioned for Florabelle to lead the way to the vault. Slocum knew this was more dangerous than anything else they could do. If Mrs. Winchester found them looking over the vault, she'd fire them both on the spot. For Slocum that wasn't such a big problem. He'd lived on a lot less than he had jingling in his pockets right now. But for Florabelle that might be the end. She had endured the death of her family well, he thought. But to be cut free from such a good job here might be more than she could tolerate in the way of misery.

"It's one of these stairs. Yes, this one. I remember." Florabelle went to the first landing, then opened a door that was hardly chest-high on Slocum. "And through here. Be very quiet. This is the part of the house where Mrs. Winchester lives."

Slocum ducked down and went through, thinking it must be nice to be so rich that carpenters would craft doors especially for your individual height and to hell with anyone else.

"The way I see it," Slocum said, "if I was the road agent, I'd strike first and get rid of anyone who might do me harm."

"You mean me, because I found this vault? Don't be silly, John. There's no way of knowing if there's even anything *in* the vault, much less if it's important. So much of this house is purest—"

Florabelle abruptly stopped speaking when Slocum grabbed her arm and pulled her into a small closet in the hall. Ahead, a dark shape moved against even darker shadows. Much of the house was brightly illuminated by gas lamps, but not this section. Whoever walked these corridors, though, moved with the lightness of a ghost—or someone who knew intimately the details of the crazy house.

"I can't make out who it is," whispered Florabelle.

"I can't, either." Slocum put his finger against Florabelle's lips to caution her to silence. They softly trod along the hardwood floors in silent pursuit of the nocturnal visitor.

A sudden rectangle of light showed a door opening and closing. The room beyond had to be brightly lit; Slocum wanted to avoid that, even though it might prove useful. Anyone inside such a room wouldn't be able to see him if he stayed in shadow.

"I don't like this, John. It's so . . . upsetting."

Slocum guessed fear was closer to what Florabelle Jackson felt now than upset. He said nothing as he pressed his ear against the door panel. He heard faint movement within the room. After the sounds faded, he hazarded a look between door and doorjamb. Slocum pulled the door open a full inch as he scanned the long, narrow room.

"It's empty!" he exclaimed.

"Whoever it was left by another door. Some of these rooms have more doors than a horse has flies," Florabelle said.

Slocum opened the door and entered the room. The door behind him was the only entrance—or exit—visible. Unlike so many other rooms, this one had no windows or other doorways.

"There must be a hidden passage somewhere," he said. "I suspected that the mansion was honeycombed with them when I heard that the butler goes out to the bell tower every night through a secret underground tunnel."

"Where?" Florabelle ran her slender fingers along the intricately carved wood wall panels. "I don't see any cracks to show where a door might open."

Slocum didn't want to waste precious minutes looking for something that he might never be able to find without tearing down the walls. "The vault. Take me to the vault. We can come back here later to do some indoor tracking."

Florabelle pointed toward the door. Slocum followed her through the maze of rooms until they came to a room that was curious even in this curious mansion. Six fireplaces lined the walls, enough to turn the room into a furnace, even in the depths of winter. And Slocum knew this part of California didn't get very cold at any time of the year.

"The central fireplace. See?" Florabelle pointed to the mantel. "It hinges. I happened to be polishing it when I bumped against it with my shoulder."

Slocum lifted the mantel and swung it back on well-oiled hinges to reveal a small recess. In the recess he grabbed a handle and tugged. The entire front of the fake fireplace moved away smoothly to reveal an elaborate Chubb safe.

"I know safes," he said in appreciation, "and this is the best I've ever seen." He examined it carefully and saw how it was built into the wall. To open this vault without the combination would require several sticks of dynamite. The only drawback to using so much explosive was the chance of destroying whatever lay within the safe.

Slocum smiled in appreciation at the risks the road agent went to for this heist. If what lay within the safe was valuable enough, maybe that made it worth the effort to dress up like a ghost.

He wondered if it was really necessary to upset Mrs. Winchester over it. Probably, he decided. The woman's fears might keep her from meddling too much.

"John?" came Florabelle's worried voice.

"What is it?" he swung around, thinking that they'd been discovered.

"You seem to know a great deal about safes—almost as if you were used to breaking into them."

This was the first time the brunette had inquired even obliquely about his past.

He wondered if he should tell her of his days with Quantrill's Raiders, of how Bloody Bill Anderson killed men and women and even children for the sick thrill of seeing them die. He had learned to hate senseless violence then, but he had also learned that violence could keep a man alive.

"I've robbed a few banks in my day," he answered.

Florabelle smiled weakly. "And I am sure you *were* the best at it. I did use the proper tense, didn't I?"

"You did. I try to be as honest as I can for at least one month out of every year."

Florabelle looked as if she didn't know whether he was joking about this. Slocum carefully closed the secret door and lowered the hinged mantelpiece. He wished he knew the true importance of what Florabelle had discovered here. It might be nothing, or it might be the key to the Indian ghost and everything else going on within the Winchester mansion.

He smiled wryly at this. *Almost* everything else. Sarah Winchester certainly provided more than her share of strangeness without dodging road agents posing as Indian spirits.

"I don't think anyone can tell we've been looking at it," Slocum said. The panel had gone back in front of the vault perfectly. After all the work he'd done in this loco house, he had to appreciate the carpentry that made such fine fits all around.

"John!" Florabelle cried. "Look. There he is again. I

think it's the same man."

She peered down the hall toward the room with the secret passage leading from it. Slocum crowded close behind Florabelle, acutely aware of her small, warm body pressed against his. He almost called an end to this wild-goose chase. Almost. He had lived with his intuition too long to ignore it now. For all that Florabelle decried it, he had a premoniton that she was in serious danger from the ghostly road agent.

He wouldn't tolerate this risk to her one moment longer than necessary, and the only way to end it was to capture or kill the man who was masquerading as the ghost.

"He's going into the same room."

Slocum tensed. He recognized the dark-clad figure. "That's Mrs. Winchester!"

"Are you sure? She's not as tall as . . . " Florabelle stopped, then laughed. "The size of the doorways is different, smaller, to accommodate her. Of course she looks bigger than she is! There's nothing of proper size to compare her to."

"Where did she go when she left the room by her secret door? And why is she returning to the room through the obvious door?" Slocum wondered.

"Oh, that's nothing, John. I heard Miss Merriam say that Mrs. Winchester walks hundreds of miles to confuse the evil spirits. She'll go in and out of a room a dozen times to be certain she's not followed. I suspect she is intent on losing any ghost intrepid enough to follow her."

"Let's find out what she has in mind. I'm interested in knowing what she has to be so secretive about."

The two of them went back into the dark hall and ran to the door. Slocum was in time to see a panel within the room snap into place. Without even pausing, he pushed into the room and went directly to the spot. Studying the area carefully revealed a hair-thin crack. Slocum's strong fingers searched the immediate area and found a small catch cunningly hidden.

The secret panel sprang open to reveal a dark, narrow corridor.

"Ahead," said Florabelle, peering past Slocum's shoulder. "I see her in another room at the end of this corridor."

Slocum was already walking down the corridor, his broad shoulders brushing the walls on either side. He and Florabelle saw Sarah Winchester don a long, dark red robe, turn the hook from which she'd taken it sharply to the right, and open still another secret door.

She stepped up and over a foot-high floorboard and vanished again.

Slocum stopped in this small anteroom and counted the robes neatly hung on other hooks. Twelve remained. Sarah Winchester's fetish for the number thirteen carried through even here—or especially here.

"John, look. She can see directly down into the kitchen from here. And into all the servants' bathrooms!"

The ceilings had been finished off in clear glass. From this vantage, Mrs. Winchester could watch most of her household staff as they went about their jobs. On one wall hung her speaking tubes. Slocum had a vision of the diminutive woman seeing some mistake being committed and immediately taking down the proper tube and chastising her victim.

"Retribution must be swift," Slocum said, shaking his head. He turned to the panel concealing the secret door and pressed his ear hard to it. Motioning Florabelle to listen also, he heard Sarah Winchester beginning her seance.

"She's invoking all the spirits of the netherworld—all the good ones, that is—to come to her aid. She thinks the

Indian ghost has finally decided to kill her after months of torment."

Slocum wished the woman would give some specific reason for her fear. If the road agent had finally come forth and threatened the woman, that meant the time was near for commission of the robbery. The Indian ghost-robber would want to keep Mrs. Winchester as occupied as possible. What better way than to play on the overwhelming fear that drove her throughout life to conduct seances, to continually build on her house, and all the rest of her strange existence?

"The poor woman!" said Florabelle. "Imagine her loneliness. How she must suffer!"

"She'd suffer more if she ever got a ghost to answer," Slocum said.

But he and Florabelle stared at one another in horror when a ghost did answer Sarah Winchester's pleas for clemency.

12

"No, John, don't!" Florabelle Jackson grabbed his arm and kept Slocum from bulling into Sarah Winchester's seance. "You'll only make things worse. She'll not like it if you interrupt her ghost while he's telling her the secrets of the netherworld."

Slocum subsided, seething inside. What Florabelle said was true. Mrs. Winchester had her own ideas about how the world ran. Talking with the spirit guides from another beyond the grave was one that he couldn't share. To her, this conversation was as real as the pungent odor of horses was to Slocum.

"Good," Florabelle said, seeing him relax a mite. "Now just listen and we might be able to do something worthwhile. We might find out more than if you confronted the ghost."

Slocum held the secret panel open enough so that he could see Mrs. Winchester's back. Her small frame hunched forward across her five-sided seance table, shrouded in the dark red ceremonial robe. Of the Indian ghost—the road agent posing as a ghost, Slocum corrected himself—he saw nothing. The flour-coated bandit stood just beyond the narrow range of vision through the doorway.

"What do the rulers of the netherworld have to tell me, O Wise and Gracious Spirit Guide?" intoned Mrs. Winchester.

"Our spirits wander the plains—doomed because of your husband's rifles!" came a booming voice. Slocum tried hard to place the voice. Like the white-dusted man's general appearance, the voice was familiar, too. But Slocum couldn't recognize it.

"I am atoning!" cried Mrs. Winchester in a voice so piteous that Slocum almost felt sorry for her. She truly believed. That made this hoax all the crueler.

"You must pay more. More!" came the bogus spirit's command.

"Tell me how. Please."

"It is not enough to build on this house," the ghost told her. "You must invite in only those who, like me, are good spirits. You must shun all the evil ones."

"But you're a red Indian!" protested Sarah Winchester. "You're one of those stalking me because you were killed by the rifle."

"My trail to the Happy Hunting Grounds is hidden. I must pay for my journey. There must be more money."

"I've already left much for you."

Florabelle clutched at Slocum's arm. He motioned her

to silence. The Indian ghost not only stole from Sarah Winchester, he was extorting money, too. Slocum wondered how much more went on that wasn't being revealed. He thought it might be a lot, especially if this road agent used the Winchester house as a base for his thieving throughout the Salinas and Santa Clara Valleys.

"Your presents to the spirit world are appreciated. Ringing the bell at the proper hour is a great boon."

"Is there anything more . . . material I can give you?" the woman asked.

"Just what I thought," said Slocum. "Here comes the demand for money." He opened the door a bit more and saw the white-floured man's arm lift. But the Indian ghost stood across the room. To reach him, Slocum would have to get past Sarah Winchester. The woman might not take kindly to having her pet spirit guide accosted.

Slocum didn't even want to think what might happen if it were revealed to her that this wasn't a ghost.

Then Slocum recoiled in surprise when the road agent told Mrs. Winchester what material thing he needed.

"We are insubstantial," said the ghost. "But you may leave a single white feather within the vault in the room of seven fires."

"That's all?" asked Mrs. Winchester.

"I need nothing from your world. I must find my path to the Happy Hunting Grounds."

"But just a feather?" the woman protested.

"A token of your faith and nothing more. In return for this, I shall tell you which of your maids has been stealing from you."

"My maids! No, I don't believe any of them would steal—" the woman began. The ghost cut her off with a wave of his hand. Slocum saw tiny clouds of flour form in the air and begin drifting on small air currents.

"Give me your token of faith, and I shall tell you which of your employees steals from you."

Florabelle gripped Slocum's arm even tighter. "Don't," she warned. "The ghost's not going to harm her. He wants something. I don't understand about the white feather, though. Why not ask for money? Or some of her jewelry? Or all of it! She's wealthy beyond any of our dreams."

Slocum had wondered about this at first, but he was beginning to see the more subtle plot that formed around him.

"Let's try to follow the ghost when he leaves. Unlike Mrs. Winchester, we know he's a fake."

They left the room with its twelve robes dangling from their hooks and went back into the hall. Slocum tried to decide how the corridors curved around and ran toward a spot where he thought he might be able to see the flour-cloaked man when he emerged from the back of the seance room.

"There! Look, John." Florabelle pointed to the floor. Small bits of flour outlined a footprint.

"He's already come by here." Slocum dropped to the floor and pressed his ear to the boards. He heard a quick, measured tread that vanished before he could get any idea where it came from.

"Which way?" Florabelle asked.

Slocum had to admit that the ghost was long gone. The man knew the interior of the building better than anyone except Sarah Winchester. Slocum puzzled over that. How did anyone come to know this place at all, much less a road agent?

"We're up against someone who's cunning and a damn sight smarter than most," Slocum admitted. He sat with his back against a wall and thought about all they'd heard. It began to fit together into a clearer picture, and one John

Slocum didn't care for.

"I don't understand about the white feather. Is that significant?" asked Florabelle.

"The feather doesn't mean a damn thing, at least as far as it goes. When Mrs. Winchester opens the safe, though, I have a notion that our ghostly friend will be watching. He'll get the combination, then steal everything from the vault. There's no other way he could get that pile of steel open."

"So he wants her to think he's just a spirit without need for money."

"If he asked for anything important, she might get suspicious. How can you doubt a ghost who offers to turn over thieving employees for a simple sign of faith like a feather?"

"He steals, then blames the servants," said Florabelle, the full plot beginning to dawn on her. "How diabolical!"

"He blames the household help, Mrs. Winchester *thanks* him, and he walks off scot free."

"We must stop him, John."

Slocum looked up at Florabelle. Her brown eyes had taken on a glow in the dimness of the hall that made her seem like a being from another world.

"I will. I owe him one hell of a lot."

"He should be turned over to the authorities, John. You mustn't harm him. That would be taking the law into your own hands. That's wrong."

Slocum kept forgetting that Florabelle had been educated back East. In the more civilized cities like New York and Boston they did things differently, they operated according to the law. Every block had a policeman on patrol, and crime wasn't all that obvious along better-class neighborhood streets. Out West, there might be long miles between sheriffs or federal marshals. Even worse, Slocum knew that Sheriff Thompson over in Los Gatos would be out of action for some time, with wounds inflicted by the man posing as the Indian ghost.

Florabelle Jackson wasn't going to like it, but if Slocum didn't personally take care of the thieving ghost, no one would.

"Should we go to the room with the vault and spy?" asked Florabelle. "We might be able to capture the ghost."

"Do you think Sarah Winchester would go within a mile of the room if anyone was inside?"

"Well, no, but . . ."

"I think our ghost will be watching, possibly through one of Mrs. Winchester's own spy holes. When she opens the vault, he'll see the combination and be able to open it whenever he wants. He won't be in the room or maybe anywhere near." Slocum remembered the complicated optical system that had let him and Buchanan spy on those in the kitchen from the third-story greenhouse. If one of those peered down into the room with the seven fireplaces, the ghost might be anywhere in the house.

"What's wrong, John? You look strange."

Slocum stood and looked at Florabelle. "We're missing something. Remember how I was worried earlier that the ghost might try to get me in trouble by leaving things he'd stolen with my things?"

"Yes. But Miss Merriam and the butler searched the bunkhouse."

"They found nothing because I wasn't the one the ghost wanted to frame. He said tonight one of the maids was doing the pilfering. We know he's responsible, so I was almost right before. Someone *is* being framed to take the blame for all the ghostly stealing, but it's not me."

"Who then?"

He looked down into her wide eyes. For a moment,

Florabelle didn't understand. Then it began to dawn on her.

"No, John, not me. Why me of all the staff?"

"I can think of several reasons. Remember what I said about the ghost trying to get to me through you? That's one damn good reason. Another is that you're the most recently hired of the household staff. If the other thefts the Indian ghost's made haven't been discovered yet, you're the logical choice—just say you'd done it all. One sneak thief, a passel of missing valuables."

"And by blaming me, he can keep on with his robbery."

"Maybe out on the road, maybe here within the house. Or he might simply move on and never even be suspected."

"We've got to catch him, John. We've got to!"

Slocum didn't ask Florabelle where she would draw the line. If she found out he was going to start carrying his Colt while he worked, she wouldn't be happy. Slocum regretted already not bringing the heavy pistol with him this night. One good shot, even if he didn't make a clean kill, would have ended the Indian ghost–road agent's career.

"Let's go back to your room," he said.

"John, there's no time for *that!*"

"Might not be a bad idea, but there's something else I want to do."

This sent a brief flare of indignation coursing through Florabelle's small frame. She stiffened and stamped her foot. "Something else?" she demanded. "And what might that be?"

"I'll show you. Then we might be able to . . ." Slocum let the words trail off. The smile returned to Florabelle's lovely face. Together they made their way through the maze, finally discovering a new set of stairs leading down to the main level.

Inside the bedroom, Florabelle looked up apprehensively at the camouflaged spy hole in the ceiling. "Do you think Mrs. Winchester will be watching?"

"Possibly, especially since her friendly spirit has told her one of you is stealing." Slocum looked around the room and finally said, "I need a mirror. I don't see one here."

Florabelle smiled and said, "In the other room. Miss Merriam furnished it. Mrs. Winchester believes that mirrors drive away the good spirits. They look into them and see that they're dead. Then they become frightened and leave."

Slocum didn't comment. This didn't strike him as any stranger than much of what went on around the Winchester mansion.

"I need the mirror. You say Miss Merriam gave you one? A good-sized mirror?"

"Not too large. I'll get it."

Slocum stayed pressed against one wall, cursing the need to avoid being in the center of the room where a watcher might see him. Florabelle returned with the mirror. He recognized it as the one she had been using when he'd sneaked into her sitting room earlier. It was only about a foot square, but it would have to do.

Slocum silently took it from the woman, then climbed up on a chair. With some difficulty he placed the mirror at a slight angle so that it reflected back from a corner of the room. As long as he stayed in the half of the room blocked by the mirror, no one could see him. With luck, anyone spying through the hole would think the room was deserted.

"Will it work?" Florabelle asked. She saw what he was trying. "It won't fool anyone long. They'll realize that both sides of the room are identical."

"Those spy portals aren't too good," Slocum said. "I

came across one up in the greenhouse."

"And you naturally tried it," said Florabelle with some disgust. "I'm disappointed in you, John."

"The one I found only looked into the kitchen."

Even Slocum knew how lame that sounded. He turned and began a thorough search of the woman's room. For a moment, Florabelle thought he was simply trying to ignore the issue. Then she understood the reason for the mirror.

"Do you really think the ghost has hidden what he's stolen in my room?"

"You're the leading candidate to be his victim," Slocum answered. He began looking behind the ornate cupboards and under the chairs to see if anything had been affixed to the seat bottoms. When Slocum turned to look up at Florabelle, he saw past her and up through the thin fabric of the covering to the four-poster bed.

"The bed," he said.

"I thought you wanted to wait, John. But if you insist..." Florabelle reached up to begin unbuttoning her blouse.

"There. Look. See the outlines?" He pointed to the canopy over the bed.

"What is it? I don't remember seeing anything there before."

"You wouldn't notice it. The light would be out when you turned in, and why look up otherwise?"

"With you in bed, there'd be no need to look any further," she said. The way her smile danced along her lips made Slocum suck in his breath and hold it. He wanted her now, but he also knew that the woman was in danger unless he finished what he'd started. After Florabelle was protected from the road agent's accusations, there'd be plenty of time for what they both wanted.

Slocum checked to be certain the mirror hid his activity,

then climbed up one post. He reached across the top of the thin muslin canopy and found the object making the shadow. He tossed down a small sterling silver serving tray. After it he found a small pouch filled with gems, four silver forks, and two large candelabra.

"These are worth a king's ransom!" Florabelle exclaimed. "But why put it all there to incriminate me?"

Slocum continued his search but found nothing else. He climbed down and sat on the chair, thinking hard. "It's worth losing it to make Mrs. Winchester accuse you of all the theft from the mansion. A few insignificant pieces wouldn't do. This has to look like the beginning of a real mother lode. When nothing more is found, you'll be guilty in Mrs. Winchester's eyes—just as the spirit said—and they'll believe you already sold the rest."

Florabelle was beside herself with anger. Slocum saw that she had gone along with him simply to keep the peace. She hadn't truly believed anyone was out to frame her. But she did now, and she was madder than a wet hen over it.

"Get a pillow case. I can't be seen with this booty." Slocum took the pillow case she fetched and stuffed in the serving tray and the rest of the loot. He fingered the pouch with the jewels, thinking what a stake this would make to get him on his way again. He reluctantly threw the chamois pouch into the pillow case, too. He had no way of telling what information the ghost was going to reveal to Mrs. Winchester once she put the feather into her vault. The ghost might give a complete inventory to strengthen the link between the spirit guide knowing all things mortal and Florabelle Jackson's guilt.

"Where are you going?" the brunette asked when she saw Slocum heft the bag and start out the door.

"To hide this somewhere else. You obviously can't keep

it, nor can I. The Indian ghost will tell Mrs. Winchester to search my belongings again when nothing's found in your room."

"I'll come with you."

He started to protest, then decided not to. Let Florabelle have a stake in her own defense. It might not completely relieve her need for getting back at the road agent—ghost, but it might keep her from doing anything stupid on her own.

Besides, Slocum didn't mind having a little company on what should prove to be an easy solution to their problems.

The pair left the house and went into the neatly kept gardens. Slocum walked until he found a distinctive ornate marble bench. He quietly slipped off the garden path and behind the bench. He dropped down and began rooting in the earth until he had a hole almost a foot deep. He put the pillow case laden with the stolen silver and jewels into the hole, then covered it.

"How does hiding the loot help, John?"

"It won't be where the ghost says. He won't know where it is. We might be able to turn the tables on him later. Don't rightly see how at the moment, but we can be on the lookout for it. What we need is an edge. Knowing he's not a ghost, knowing the tricks he's played on Mrs. Winchester, and now hiding all he's planted on you ought to be enough."

They silently returned to the house, following a different path through the garden to be sure no one had spotted them hiding the loot. That would have been as bad as having the spirit accuse them—maybe worse, from Slocum's viewpoint.

"Do we have to go inside right away?" asked Florabelle, stopping him at the edge of the garden. Slocum didn't want to. Staying outside on such a fine spring night with such a lovely woman looked to him to be more exciting, but he shook his head.

"We've got to play this hand with what cards we have. We're up against a dangerous outlaw. Don't ever forget that."

"I won't, John." Florabelle looked up into his green eyes. "You know what I think, John? I think *you're* the dangerous one. This road agent doesn't know what kind of trouble he's crossed in you."

Slocum kissed her. They stood locked in each other's arms for several minutes, then Slocum broke off. "You're going to be missed if you stay out too much longer."

Florabelle sighed. "You're right. That trick with the mirror is one I'm going to use again, though. That was truly clever on your part, John." Their eyes locked. How he wanted her! But they both had jobs to do and they couldn't be caught together.

Just as they entered the long corridor leading to Florabelle's room, Slocum stopped and pulled the brunette to one side. He silently pointed to a pair of dark figures entering Florabelle's room.

"The game's starting in earnest now," he said. "That was Miss Merriam. I reckon the man with her is the butler. They've come to search your room."

"Let's not disappoint them further," said Florabelle, her mouth set in a determined line. She took a certain amount of glee out of outwitting the Indian ghost, Slocum saw. He wanted to warn her about getting too cocky, but he held his peace.

"You go on. It's better if they don't see me with you. You know what Mrs. Winchester thinks about her household staff mingling with the carpenters."

"Any unmarried female with any unmarried male," said Florabelle. She giggled like a schoolgirl. "It's good that I never learned *that* lesson in school. Oh, how upset Mrs. Murchison would be!"

Slocum waited outside as Florabelle went in. He heard every word uttered inside the bedroom perfectly.

"Why, Miss Merriam, whatever are you doing?" Florabelle exclaimed. "How dare you go through my belongings! This is most uncalled for!"

"Mrs. Winchester has had a premonition," Miss Merriam said. "She thinks you have taken some of her valuables."

"The idea! Well, I have nothing to hide. Go on, search. I am honest and wish only to clear my name of this black spot."

Slocum thought Florabelle laid on the innocence too thick, but Miss Merriam apparently expected it. She apologized even as she gave the butler orders to continue searching. After ten minutes they had discovered nothing.

The Chinese butler finally said, "Canopy of bed. Let me check." Slocum heard muffled grunts as the man climbed onto a chair—probably the same one Slocum himself had used—and searched. Predictably, he found nothing.

"I am sorry, Miss Jackson," said Margaret Merriam. "My aunt has odd notions at times, as you probably already know." Slocum barely heard the secretary's next remark because it came in a low whisper. ". . . and don't let my aunt see that mirror you have in front of the spy hole. You know how she is about looking glasses."

Slocum ducked into a doorway and pressed himself flat as Miss Merriam and the butler left Florabelle's room, then walked briskly away. He paused, considering what to do next. A slow smile crossed his face. He had told Florabelle to wait until matters were well in hand.

They seemed to be now. He slipped into the room to spend an enjoyable few hours until he had to show up for his midnight work shift.

13

"That's damned sloppy work, Slocum. Do it over. You keep this up and I'll see that the old lady fires you."

Slocum turned and looked at Clarence Hormel. The foreman stood in the shadows, arms crossed and slumped over. All during the shift he had been peering over Slocum's shoulder and making insulting comments that caused Slocum to boil inside. But Slocum had said nothing up till now. For some reason, Hormel was riding him hard, trying to prod Slocum into a fight by complaining about the quality of the work.

Slocum dropped the heavy claw-hammer back into the leather strap on his tool belt and settled it all into place. He had stuck his Colt inside his shirt. It made a bulge, but not too obvious. He would have a devil of a time trying to get it out and into action in a hurry, but if he had the time, he would also have a goodly amount of firepower that he had been lacking before.

"Is there something eating away at your gut, Hormel?" he asked. "You been after me all night long for no good reason, and I'm getting mighty tired of it."

"You're doing poor work. We don't stand for that. Mrs. Winchester pays good money. Too good in your case. You don't have the skill to do the work she needs."

"Stuff a rag in it, Hormel," Benny Buchanan spoke up. "Slocum here's as good as any man you got on this shift. And maybe that includes me. He's a hell of a sight better'n you are with a hammer.''

"I can have the pair of you fired."

"So do it. Leastways then we won't have to listen to your damn yammering. Now get on out of here and let us do our work. We can have this finished in an hour." Buchanan swung his hammer against a bare plank. It landed with a heavy thud that emphasized his mood.

Slocum thought Hormel would argue. Instead, the foreman spun and stalked from the room. He watched him go, not sure what had got into the man. Before tonight, Hormel had left him alone. In fact, Hormel had seemed afraid of him. But now the foreman took every opportunity to cut Slocum down in front of the other men.

Slocum mulled over this. He and Hormel had never been alone together. Hormel had taken to mumbling and standing in the shadows whenever Slocum was around. The idea that Slocum had seen the man somewhere else came back even stronger than before. He still didn't remember the circumstances, but he would. Slocum touched the Colt inside his shirt. When he remembered for certain, he knew he'd probably have to use the gun.

The niggling sensation had that kind of importance attached to the remembering.

"He's sure bein' a pain tonight, ain't he?" said Buchanan. "Wonder why?"

"It's as if he wants to get rid of me but is afraid to come right out and do anything about it."

"He's a mean one, Slocum. I seen him take an axe handle to a fellow twice his size. Hormel beat the livin' daylights out of him. Woulda killed him, 'cept three others pulled him off in time. But you haven't done nothin' to make him mad. Not unless you been sneakin' around doin' things when I wasn't looking."

"You don't miss much, do you?"

"The only way," said Buchanan, a broad grin on his face, "that you don't ride on into San Jose with the rest of us to find a good whore-house is that you got something on the fire around here. That filly you came ridin' in with, what's her name now?"

"You old fraud. You know what it is."

"Florabelle. Right purty name, Florabelle. Knew a woman back in St. Louis named Florabelle. Best damn woman I ever had. Think it's got something to do with the name?"

"Doubt it." Slocum fell silent as Buchanan began a long-winded discussion about the women he'd known and bedded. By the end of their shift, Slocum was positive Buchanan had screwed every female west of the Mississippi twice.

The shift ended just as Slocum and Buchanan finished the room they were working on. The walls and windows had been framed in and other crews would now do the finishing work. Bone weary, they dropped their tool belts in the equipment shed and walked toward the bunkhouse.

Buchanan looked at Slocum and muttered to himself.

"What's that?" asked Slocum.

"I was just thinkin' on men what carried guns to work. That spirit roamin' the house ain't got you spooked, now does he?"

"Something like that."

"Mrs. Winchester don't like her workmen carryin' guns."

"I don't think Hormel does either, but for a different reason." Slocum stared ahead to where Hormel stood by the bunkhouse door. He was arguing with a man who was hunched over in obvious pain.

"Who's that?" Buchanan asked.

"Seems the Los Gatos sheriff's come to pay us a visit," said Slocum. He kept walking until he got even with the two men. "Morning, Sheriff Thompson."

Thompson, pale and drawn, looked up at Slocum. No hint of pleasure showed on his weatherbeaten face. In point of plain fact, Slocum wondered how the man had gotten here without dying from the pain he so obviously endured.

"You, Slocum—you're the one I came to talk to. You can leave us, Mr. Hormel."

Hormel's anger rose but he stalked off without a word.

"What can I do for you, Sheriff? Must be important. You don't look up to traveling around much."

"That damn road agent's been at work again. Held up a Wells, Fargo stage only yesterday. I want him, Slocum. I want him so bad I can taste it." Coughing wracked the man's body and he hunched over even more.

"You don't look like you could fight a week-old kitten and stand any good chance of winning," Slocum said.

"I got my duty to do. No one else's going to catch him. Upped the reward to two hundred dollars."

"Riding out here to see me has tired you out," said Slocum. "Want to sit down?" He indicated a nearby marble bench. Gratefully, the sheriff collapsed onto it. The man's gray pallor hinted at the full extent of his wounds.

"You see anything what might be useful to catchin' this scoundrel?" asked Thompson. "I hankered after that reward myself, but now I'm willing to give it to any bounty-hunting son of a bitch who can bring in the road agent."

Slocum figured that intense pressure was being applied by Wells, Fargo and Company to stop the bandit. Maybe even the citizens of Los Gatos were hot to lynch the road agent. Slocum wasn't against such a necktie party, not after what had been done to him. The crease across his shoulder had healed but the memory of his fine strawberry roan being shot dead and the crisp greenbacks being taken still caused a cold lump to form in the pit of his stomach. What had been done to the sheriff only added to the intensity of his feelings against the outlaw.

"I want him, too, Sheriff."

"You better do something about it. You were out there with me. You know how dangerous he is. You got to." Thompson's tone was close to accusing, as if Slocum was the road agent. "It takes a dangerous man to catch another one. You got to get him."

Slocum decided that Thompson was too badly injured to fight effectively and that this was the sheriff's way of asking for help. It still rankled, but Slocum could almost understand.

"We both want him, Sheriff. He can't keep up his thieving ways forever."

"Doing a damn good job so far. You see to it, Slocum. You see to it or there'll be hell to pay!"

Sheriff Thompson rose and shuffled off. Slocum didn't see how the man could ride a horse in his condition. When he heard the rattle of wheels, he knew that the sheriff had

come from Los Gatos in a carriage. Slocum puzzled over
the man's stupidity, then decided it was more determination
and pride. Not much in the way of crime happened in Los
Gatos. Now that an outlaw had started plying his trade
along the road through the entire length of the Santa Clara
Valley, Thompson felt obligated to earn his meager salary.

Slocum knew the lawman was outgunned and out-
classed by the road agent, and experienced a pang of pity
for the sheriff. He went into the bunkhouse to find Hormel
arguing with Benny Buchanan.

"I don't give two hoots what you want, Hormel. I got to
ride the hedges for Yamaguchi. He's one of them in charge
around here. Not like you."

"I'm the damned foreman!" shouted Hormel. "And
you'll do as I say or I'm gonna fire you."

"Promises, promises," Buchanan snorted. "You ain't
got the authority. Only the secretary or Yamaguchi can hire
or fire in this crazy house. And the gardener tells me to
ride patrol, so I ride patrol."

Buchanan started to leave. Hormel grabbed him by the
shoulder and spun him around. Buchanan staggered. Slocum caught him.

"You stay out of this, Slocum," snarled Hormel.

"Didn't know I was in it." Slocum tried to get past Buchanan to his own bunk. Hormel turned on him. A hard
palm slammed into his shoulder, knocking him back. Slocum grimaced. His back still gave him twinges now and
again.

"I'm speaking to you, Slocum. Are you going to stay
out of it?"

Slocum saw that Buchanan wasn't inclined to help. The
man backed off, headed for the door, and vanished. Hormel squarely faced Slocum.

"Didn't want in it, but since you put me here, Hormel, I might as well speak my mind. You've been riding me hard for the past few shifts for no good reason."

"No good reason, he says!" shouted Hormel. "Listen to this jackass! The man's slacking off, making work for the rest of his shift, and he says no good reason."

Slocum half expected it, but he couldn't move fast enough to avoid the full impact of Hormel's fist. The man swung flatfooted and this saved Slocum from a broken cheekbone. Slocum fell heavily onto his back. Instinctively, his hand went for the Colt inside his shirt.

Slocum never reached it. Hormel's booted foot came hard for his head and Slocum had to roll under a nearby bunk to avoid it. His shirt caught on a nail in the floor and ripped. By the time he came out on the other side of the bunk, his gun had come free.

He lifted the heavy Colt, more to deter the rampaging foreman than to kill him. Hormel reacted by diving atop Slocum. The man's crushing weight forced Slocum to drop the gun. The pair rolled over and over until they crashed against a footlocker.

"Hey, go outside!" came an angry voice. "No fightin' in the bunkhouse. You know the rules. Don't give a damn if you are foreman, Hormel. You got to go outside."

Slocum stood, not wanting to continue this pointless fight. Hormel's heavy fist shot out again, missing his chin and catching him high on the shoulder. Off balance, Slocum spun hard and crashed into the wall. Another punch landed in his kidneys. Slocum gasped as a sheet of red pulled over his eyes. Everything spun wildly around him as Slocum sank to his knees.

"He's had enough, Hormel. Christ, look at him. He's about out on his feet."

"He pulled a gun on me, Mason. I got to make sure he don't do that again."

Slocum had begun to recover when Hormel hit him again. This time the punch came hard and on target to his belly. Slocum doubled over, but pain was beginning to mean nothing. The red fire of pain turned into cold anger. Slocum threw his arms out and circled Hormel's body. Powerful legs kicked out to drive against the wall and propel both men into the center of the bunkhouse.

Hormel was caught off guard. The pair crashed to the floor, Slocum with his shoulder squarely planted in Hormel's belly. The air gushed from the foreman's lungs.

By the time Hormel could gasp his curses, Slocum had recovered.

"Mason wants us to go outside. I see no reason not to oblige him. Unless you don't fight men who're ready for you, Hormel."

"You son of a bitch!"

The foreman roared and charged Slocum, but this time he had no advantage of surprise. Slocum didn't try to halt the bull's rush. Instead, he waited, judged, then moved to his right, one hand grabbing Hormel's groping right wrist and the other the back of his shirt collar. With a mighty heave, Slocum threw Hormel out the door to land on the neatly tended path.

"That's the way to go, Slocum. The bastard deserved it." Several others in the bunkhouse expressed similar sentiments. But Slocum saw that none of them turned away. They knew the fight was just starting, and they didn't want to miss a second of it. Slocum followed Hormel out and stood, feet squarely planted and ready for a real fight.

Hormel came at him again, once more rushing. Slocum's left went out in a short, powerful jab. He caught the charging foreman on the side of the head. Hormel grunted harshly and kept coming. He caught Slocum in a bear hug, lifting him off the ground. Pain jolted Slocum as Hormel applied pressure.

Everything was wavering before him as if he stared through a desert's heat shimmer. Slocum knew he had only seconds to act before he passed out. He slammed the flats of his hands onto Hormel's ears. The foreman shrieked in pain and dropped his victim. Slocum fell to one knee, then used the power of his legs as well as his arm to drive a right fist deep into Hormel's well-muscled gut.

"Gonna kill you, Slocum. Can't do this to me," Hormel panted.

Slocum feinted, dodged a clumsy blow, and got a left into Hormel's belly. He kept hammering away at the man's midsection, knowing he had to weaken Hormel quick. Slocum felt his strength draining fast.

"Call it off, Hormel. You don't need to do this. We've got no quarrel."

"Son of a bitch!" Hormel shrieked and attacked again. Slocum took a light punch to the side of the jaw, jerked to one side, and landed two hard punches to Hormel's gut. A still harder third one to the stomach doubled the foreman over.

Slocum saw his chance and took it. He brought his knee up into Hormel's face, swung with all the remaining strength he had, and landed a final blow on the man's left temple. The foreman crumpled to the ground, twitching weakly, blood oozing from a swollen and split lip. Slocum was scarcely in better shape. He tottered a bit, then sat down on the marble bench where he and Sheriff Thompson had talked.

"Good riddance," came one man's comment. Another

one said, "Hormel's always bragging. This ought to take the wind out of his sails." Still another added, "Maybe now we can get some sleep."

Slocum wanted to laugh. This fight had started for no good reason other than Hormel's argument with Buchanan, and Benny had quickly disappeared once the fists started flying. It had boiled over to him. And all the others in the bunkhouse wanted was to go to sleep. Thinking on it, that was all he wanted to do, too.

He got to his feet and walked unsteadily to his bunk. Someone had put his Colt on his pillow. He tucked it underneath, then climbed into bed. Hand resting on the butt of the gun, Slocum was asleep in seconds.

14

Slocum didn't awaken until Benny Buchanan returned from guard duty, cursing a blue streak and slamming his fist into anything that didn't move out of his way. Slocum opened one puffy eye, his hand still wrapped around the butt of his gun. He relaxed when he saw the other man was alone.

"What's ailing you?" Slocum asked. "You sound like you ate a tree full of green apples."

"It's that sidewinder Hormel. He just gave me hell when I came in. Looks like you gave him hell earlier, though. His face was all swole up and he could hardly talk. You split his lip but good and he's got a shiner that's not goin' away for a month of Sundays."

Slocum sat up in the bunk, his long legs dangling over

the side. "A lot of help you were. He starts a fight with you, then you let me finish it for you."

"Wasn't like that, Slocum, and you know it," said Buchanan.

"So tell me how it was."

"Yamaguchi told me to get right on out to patrol. You know how he is. He woulda fired me if I hadn't been on duty."

Slocum said nothing to this. It sounded lame and both men knew it.

"See anything worth mentioning?" asked Slocum.

"While I was out ridin' the hedges?" Buchanan snorted derisively. "Never do. Can't see why Yamaguchi wants to pay me to be out there. Prefer it if I could get some rest."

"Didn't even see Sheriff Thomspon?" asked Slocum.

"That lawman from Los Gatos? Naw, he was gone by the time I started. You and him talked and he musta left before I saddled up."

"Get some rest," Slocum advised. "We've only got a few hours before it'll be time to pound a few more nails."

"Right." Buchanan dropped onto his bunk and soon was snoring. Slocum stared at the man for a few seconds, then dropped lightly to the floor. He stretched and found himself in surprisingly good shape after the hard fight. His knuckles were a mite skinned, but other than this minor injury, he felt damned good. His back wasn't even acting up. Fisticuffs must be good for a man, he reflected.

Slocum tucked his Colt inside his shirt, then let the torn fabric blouse out a bit to hide the pistol's bulge. He left the bunkhouse and walked into the cool spring night. He began to wander aimlessly, hardly seeing the beauty of the grounds Yamaguchi kept so well. His mind worked on everything that had happened until he started to get a headache. But pieces of the puzzle refused to come together for him. One vital fact eluded him, and no matter how much he chewed on it, he failed to come up with a good answer.

Slocum stopped just short of an older portion of the mansion and looked up into a well-lit second-story window. In the room he saw a figure moving—a maid going about her chores.

When she came to the window and looked out, Slocum waved. It was Florabelle.

"John!" she said in happy surprise. "How long have you been down there?"

"Not long. I was just trying to get everything squared away in my head."

"I heard you had a fight with Mr. Hormel. I'm sorry I couldn't come to see you."

"We shouldn't be talking like this. Miss Merriam might come along, or Mrs. Winchester."

"You're right. Stay right where you are and I'll be down in a minute."

"No, Florabelle, you don't . . ." But she had vanished from the window and reappeared at a nearby door. The only problem facing her was the lack of stairs connected to the second-story door.

"Careful," Slocum said. "That's a long drop." She had gone to a door that opened into thin air.

"Can you catch me if I fall?" She stood close enough to the edge so that her skirt flared in the soft breeze blowing through the garden. Slocum saw a nice turn of ankle and something of the fine, sleek legs beneath that skirt.

"Reckon I can."

"Good, then here I come!"

Slocum jumped forward, arms outstretched when he saw what she had in mind. Florabelle had twisted around in the door, feet free. She lowered herself a few inches, then kicked out and fell so that he could catch her. His arms circled her small, firm body, but the force of her fall was almost more than Slocum could stand. He stumbled and went to his knees, but he didn't drop her.

The brunette got to her feet, patted her hair into place, then reached over and ran her fingertips along Slocum's upper arms. "You're so strong," she said in a seductive whisper.

"You damn near killed me jumping like that."

"I don't think so. No one dies like that. But what about..." Florabelle bent over and whispered quickly in Slocum's ear, then lightly bit it.

"No one's died from too much loving, either," he said, answering her question. "But that'd be a good way to go."

"Let's not die, John, let's live!"

She took his hand and pulled him to his feet. Skipping like a young schoolgirl, Florabelle took off across the grounds. He made a grab for her but she deftly avoided his hands. She made a mocking gesture to let him know that getting her wouldn't be *that* easy. Like a butterfly, Florabelle ran through the garden, keeping just inches ahead of Slocum. By the time they had reached the barn behind the mansion, they were both breathless.

Florabelle fell into his arms, her head resting against his broad chest.

"You excite me so, John. It's not natural what you do to my emotions." She tilted back her head. He saw moonlight reflect off her pert, upturned nose. Florabelle's delicately boned, lovely face turned to liquid silver in the light and her eyes shone brilliantly. "I want you. Now."

He kissed her, his lips brushing almost delicately over hers. Florabelle's tongue slipped between her parted lips, played across Slocum's, then boldly intruded into his mouth. Tongues rolling over and over, imitating what would soon be happening later, the kiss deepened. Slocum finally had to come up for air.

"We ought to get out of sight. Wouldn't do to have Mr. Yamaguchi find us together."

"He just doesn't want his plants to get the wrong idea by watching two humans making love," said Florabelle. "Might confuse the poor man's Swedish ivy."

"I'm not confused as to what I want," said Slocum. He kissed her again, this time harder. Their lips crushed and their bodies pressed together. Slocum's hand roved up and down the small woman's back, touching here and there, stimulating, stroking, finally coming to rest so that he cupped her firm buttocks.

She moved even closer, her hips grinding slightly. Slocum felt himself getting harder until it became uncomfortable. He tightened his grip on her and lifted her entirely off the ground. Florabelle squealed with joy as he swung her around and deposited her just inside the barn door.

In the back stalls, two horses shifted nervously at the sounds. One tried kicking at its stall but soon subsided.

"We're frightening the animals," Florabelle said.

"Not as much as we will be soon."

Florabelle slipped from his arms and ducked when he grabbed for her. She was as frisky as a filly. He recognized in her the need to frolic a mite before they got down to serious lovemaking. And, truth to tell, he wasn't against it himself.

Like two children, they ducked and dodged one another until Slocum slipped and fell backward into a pile of hay. "Help me up," he called, stretching out his hand to her.

"No way will you catch me with an old trick like that!" Florabelle said, hands on flaring hips. Slocum saw the woman's silhouette and began to stiffen even more. He groaned. This was ceasing to be fun and starting to hurt. He needed her. He needed her bad.

"Don't go running off, Belle," he said. "Come here."

"No, up in the loft. Up where we can look down on the entire world!" Florabelle turned and darted for a wooden ladder leading to the loft. Slocum levered himself to his feet and lurched after her. He missed her delicately turned ankle by a fraction of an inch. Cursing under his breath, he started up the ladder after her.

"There's no place to run now," he said with mock menace. "I've got you cornered!"

She didn't try to escape. She greeted him openly, warmly. He buried his face in her soft dark hair and smelled the fragrance of it, of her lips and neck and body.

"Now, John, now. I can't wait any longer."

Slowly, one button at a time, he undid her blouse. Her frilly undergarments were shucked off to expose the firm white mounds of her breasts. In the moonlight coming in through an opened loft door, Florabelle's nipples took on the look of something exotic. Slocum kissed each in turn, even as he worked off her skirt.

"Give me a few seconds," he said. He ripped off his shirt, all pretense gone for drawing out her pleasure. He desperately needed her.

Slocum tossed aside his Colt, then his trousers. Florabelle said nothing as she came to him, her arms circling his neck, her legs parting to go on either side of his hips. She kept walking and Slocum fell backward into a pile of hay.

Florabelle shivered all over as she reached between their bodies and found his hot length. She gripped it, stroked over it quickly, then lifted herself up enough to swing him under her. She relaxed and slid down around his hardened column.

For a moment, neither said a word. Neither moved. Neither could believe the extreme pleasure this simple act afforded.

Slocum reached up and cupped both of Florabelle's apple-sized breasts. He kneaded them like dough, moving them in small circles, then in larger and larger ones. He felt the nipples pulsing with added blood until both were as hard as tiny pebbles.

"I can't stay still, John. You fill me up so. I can't stay still!"

The woman began lifting herself upward. Just when Slocum was afraid he would slip from her tight warmth, Florabelle reversed direction. Up and down she went. Slocum got the idea. He began guiding her in the motion he liked best by the pressure on her breasts. Florabelle twisted slowly from side to side, sat up, bent forward, began changing position—all the while maintaining the rhythmic movement.

But Slocum knew he couldn't endure much more. "Faster," he said. "Go faster!" His hips began lifting off the hay to meet her downward-driving groin. They crushed together harder and harder until passion took total control of them both.

Gasping, moaning, they came. Florabelle let out a low moan and sagged forward. Slocum took her in his arms, his loins weak and empty. They lay together, her atop him for some time. Then Slocum turned and rolled Florabelle into the hay beside him so that he could better look at her. The moonlight danced across her hair and turned her into something magical.

"It gets better 'n' better," he said.

"I know. I wanted to—" Slocum reached over and pressed his hand across her mouth before she could finish. His sharp ears had detected movement in the barn below.

And that movement didn't come from restless horses.

Florabelle nodded to show she understood. They began getting back into their clothes in case they had to sneak

out. Slocum finished before Florabelle but couldn't find his
Colt. He searched in the hay for it, but the pistol had vanished.

"John, look!"

Slocum peered through a large crack in the loft to the
tackroom. The dark figure entering the tackroom looked
familiar.

"The Indian ghost!"

"Might be," he allowed. "But we can't be sure. Might
just be one of the hands come to work on his gear." Slocum
didn't know if he considered it natural or not for the Winchester mansion to run a full twenty-four hours a day.
Straining, he was able to hear the pounding of hammers as
the carpenters worked away at building the monstrosity of
a house for Sarah Winchester.

"It's him. I know it!" Florabelle insisted.

Slocum wasn't going to argue. He moved so that he
could get a better look at what went on below. The shadowy figure had entered the tackroom and lit a lantern.
Sounds of a barrel top falling onto the floor echoed through
the barn. Then came silence.

"Look for my gun. I lost it in the hay," he told Florabelle. The brunette scrambled around on hands and knees
looking for the gun. She didn't find it and soon gave up.

"I want to see," he said. "You keep watch." Slocum
tried to find the gun. When he again heard movement
below, he gave up the search in favor of peering down. A
shadowy man dressed in conventional clothing had entered
the tackroom. A white ghost decked out in Indian breech-
clout and complete with jagged, dark stripes of war paint
on chest and face emerged.

"I *was* right," Florabelle exclaimed.

The ghost stopped and looked around, head cocked to
one side. He'd heard the woman's outburst.

Slocum cursed his inability to find his fallen pistol. One easy shot from the Colt would have ended the charade once and for all. He rose, steadied himself on a post, and prepared to launch himself at the road agent—ghost.

As if the ghost truly possessed supernatural powers, he turned and ran for the side of the barn, moving so that Slocum would be unable to jump him.

"He's below us," said Florabelle. "There. I can see him there!"

Slocum dropped to his hands and knees and peered through the same crack in the loft floor. He saw nothing.

"Find my gun. I'm going to make sure he doesn't leave by the door." Slocum ran to the loft door and swung out. Below, the main barn doors were slightly ajar. The ghost was nowhere to be seen, but he hadn't left the barn yet.

"John, here it is!"

Florabelle carried the heavy pistol in both hands. She passed it over to him as if she'd picked up a live rattlesnake.

He took the familiar weight in his hand, settled himself, then swung out on the loft arm. He lowered himself via the rope and pulley and came to the ground just in front of the doors.

"He's still in the stall. He hasn't left it," the woman called to him. "Be careful, John."

He didn't need that advice. The outlaw masquerading as the Indian ghost had showed himself to be cunning and cruel. Slocum wasn't going to underestimate him now. Every sense alert to the slightest motion, sound, or presence, Slocum entered the barn, gun barrel swiveling left and right. Only the sounds from the horses came to him. He advanced, searching each stall, left and right, as he went to be sure he hadn't been mistaken about which one the ghost hid in.

Approaching the stall where he'd last seen the ghost, Slocum spun and held the cocked Colt in front of him, ready to fire.

He didn't believe what he saw.

"John, did you capture him?" came Florabelle's eager voice from above.

Slocum straightened from his gunfighter's crouch and let down the hammer on his Colt.

"No," he called back. "The ghost has vanished into thin air."

The empty stall mocked him.

15

John Slocum didn't know what to do. He stood there in the middle of the barn staring into an empty stall. Cautiously entering the stall, he began poking around, unsure of what he might find. It might have been possible for the ghost to slip over the top of one stall and into another, but Slocum hadn't seen him when he checked all the other stalls getting to this one.

The Indian ghost had vanished into thin air, just like a real spirit.

"Where is he, John? What happened?" Florabelle came rushing down the ladder, her skirts flying and her blouse flapping open where she hadn't properly rebuttoned it.

"He got away. How, I don't know. But he's gone." Slocum took a deep breath. "I know where to find him, though."

"The house?"

"Why else would he get into his disguise?" Slocum asked. "He is going to meet with Mrs. Winchester again."

"More craziness about feathers in the safe?" Florabelle shook her head, sending bits of straw sailing from her hair. She unconsciously reached up to brush it out.

"He wants something from Mrs. Winchester and he hasn't got it yet."

"Maybe she didn't put the feather in the vault. Or maybe he couldn't read the combination when she worked the dial."

"That's possible, Belle, but I doubt it. Our flour-covered friend hasn't made that kind of mistake yet. When he concocted this Indian ghost scheme, he must have been pretty damned sure he could see her opening the safe."

Florabelle looked all around, then went into the tackroom. "No sign of him. Not even his clothes."

"Damn, I forgot about his clothes," said Slocum. "He must change here, go into the mansion, then return. But why the barn? Why not somewhere else?"

"Who's going to see him in the middle of night?" asked Florabelle.

"That's not the question. Why take the chance of being seen going all the way from the barn to the house? Why not change in one of the mansion's unused rooms? No one checks them out regularly. Hell," Slocum said, smiling, "nobody even knows where they all are."

"So he's a ghost haunting the gardens, too."

Slocum didn't answer, but he doubted this. Yamaguchi prowled the gardens day and night. Slocum had no idea when the Japanese gardener slept, if he ever did. But Miss Merriam and the others on the staff were alerted to the ghost's prowling about—and they didn't believe in spirits like Mrs. Winchester did. They'd be more inclined to take a shotgun to the flour-coated fake.

Slocum prowled through the small, well-kept tackroom, searching for the discarded clothing that ought to be there. It wasn't. Slocum scratched his head. Something eluded him and he couldn't figure out what it was.

"Let's get back to the mansion," Slocum said. "I got to be at work soon—and you should be right now."

"That's not it, John," said Florabelle. "You know that the ghost is getting ready to appear for Mrs. Winchester and you want to track him down alone. Well, I want to go with you!"

"Florabelle, please. This is going to be dangerous."

"You're trying to say that you'll shoot down our flour-covered fake spirit the instant you see him. That's one reason I want to be along. You need someone to stop you from doing such a damnfool thing that'll only cause us all a world of misery."

"That's one reason," Slocum said. "What's the other?"

Florabelle's brown eyes danced with excitement. "I don't want to miss out on one instant of this!"

This reason he could approve. "We'd better hurry," said Slocum. "Our 'haint' must already be in the house, and it'll take us a while figuring out how to get to Mrs. Winchester's seance room."

Slocum was acutely aware of Florabelle's presence all the way to the house. She pressed close, her warm body rubbing seductively against his. Florabelle could only distract him, and if that happened at the wrong instant, they both might die. Still, Slocum couldn't easily chase off the woman. In a way, she deserved to be along. The ghost had tried to frame her for the theft of a considerable amount of silver and jewels. She deserved to see the ghost brought to justice—or brought to the ground with a couple slugs in his head.

Slocum wasn't forgetting what had been done to him out on the road. That roan had been a damn fine horse.

They wandered through the twisting halls of the mansion until Slocum held Florabelle back, motioning her to silence.

Ahead, down a corridor so narrow that Slocum's shoulders brushed both walls, he saw a small figure moving in the shadows. It could be no one but Sarah Winchester.

"She's going into the secret cloakroom," Florabelle said in a low voice.

They followed slowly, knowing how the woman often doubled back to evade her ghostly pursuers. Slocum figured that Mrs. Winchester would have made a fine scout if she ever left this house and got out onto the range where such skills really mattered.

Slocum pushed open the door and stepped high over the baseboard into the robe room. Beyond the secret panel sat Sarah Winchester, already muttering her mystical incantations to invoke a spirit guide and peering into her crystal ball for guidance.

Slocum drew his Colt and waited. After ten minutes, nothing happened. He began to get edgy. Then Mrs. Winchester's voice rose and her words became more distinct.

"I have delivered the white feather as a token of my faith. Where are you, O Great and Gracious One?"

"John, let's see if we can capture the ghost at the vault," Florabelle whispered.

Slocum thought it might be too late, but he nodded. They slipped from the room after closing the secret panel. Slocum had pretty well memorized the path to the fireplace room. He checked the hall and the surrounding rooms to be sure the ghost hadn't laid a trap for them, then entered. It took a few seconds to sing back the mantle and check the hidden vault.

"The door's ajar!" exclaimed Florabelle. "He's already beaten us to the treasure."

Slocum knelt and looked at the insides of the vault. A single feather lay in the center.

"Whatever he wanted, I don't think he got it from this safe. See the way the dust has accumulated? The feather's on top of it. I don't think Sarah Winchester ever used this vault."

"There are five other vaults," said Florabelle. "Least-ways, that's what Miss Merriam said once when we found this one by accident. She didn't sound as if she approved, either."

"Probably makes her bookkeeping too complicated," said Slocum, his mind on other matters. "The ghost might keep Mrs. Winchester opening safes until he can get into one with real booty."

"We should listen to her seance, then."

"Let's try to find where the Indian ghost came out the last time." Slocum held out less chance of stopping the ghost now, but he wanted a better look at him. Identify him and everything else fell into place. He might not have enough evidence to turn him over to the sheriff, but then Slocum wasn't looking to build a legal case.

All he wanted was to be certain in his own mind. He would save the sheriff the expense of a jury trial.

With all the care he would take in tracking a wounded buck, Slocum examined the corridors, depending on Flora-belle to keep track of where they turned. This wasn't like a forest where certain landmarks might be located. The halls took on a sameness in spite of their convoluted twistings that confused the unwary.

"Here," he said. "Flour." Slocum looked up in surprise. Half a faint footprint came from the wall. He examined the wall and discovered a tiny spring catch at shoulder level—above eye level for someone of Sarah Winchester's height—that popped open another secret door. Stairs spiraled downward. The fetid air blowing into his face indicated an opening near horses.

"It goes into the barn," said Florabelle, putting into words what Slocum had already decided. "This is how the ghost got away. He opened a secret panel in the barn and came directly here."

Slocum crawled off on his hands and knees, following the faint imprints on the wood floor. Now and again he found traces of sweat-dampened flour that kept him on the proper path. The trail led into a room he had never seen before.

Slocum looked questioningly at Florabelle, who only shrugged. This was new territory for both of them. Just when they thought they were learning how the house was laid out, new confusions cropped up.

Colt firmly in hand, Slocum opened the door cautiously. The room looked down onto the deserted kitchen through a series of windows tilted so that those below couldn't see anyone spying on them.

Slocum prowled the room, checking the other doors. Two opened into blank walls. The third opened into a room he thought to be near Mrs. Winchester's seance chamber. The flour trail led in this direction, so Slocum followed.

"How does he know this place so much better than we do?" asked Florabelle.

"I have my suspicions on that point," said Slocum. "We're going to find out real quick if I'm right. Listen."

Muffled voices came through one thin wall. Slocum pressed his ear against the plaster and heard Mrs. Winchester and someone else talking. It had to be the elusive ghost.

"John, here!" whispered Florabelle. She had found the way into the seance chamber used by the ghost.

The entire wall slid to one side. It took both Slocum and Florabelle to slide the panel shut behind them, but once inside they had a clear view of all that went on. The ghost stood five feet from Sarah Winchester, almost glowing with his flour covering. The black war paint made the face seem even more deathlike. In one hand he held a short war lance and in the other a small hide shield. The ghost brandished both as he spoke.

"There will be other tokens of your devotion," the Indian ghost said.

"But what, O Spirit Guide?"

"I require another feather. In the vault where the windows look to the rising sun. A gray feather from the high-flying eagle!"

"Why do you test me in this way?" Sarah Winchester sounded almost irritated.

"The souls of those braves who have died require it," said the phony ghost.

Florabelle nudged Slocum and said softly, "It doesn't sound like the same man. The words are coming out muffled, even mushy, as if he had rocks in his mouth."

Slocum smiled without humor. He knew the identity of the ghost—and it didn't surprise him in the least.

"It's hard talking when you've been in a fight and got your lip split. And that black war paint hides one beauty of a shiner."

"Fight? What fight?" It slowly dawned on Florabelle. "That's Clarence Hormel!"

"Of course it is," said Slocum. "Who else could possibly know the layout of this house as well as the building foreman? He's probably got access to all the blueprints. Might even be how he came across the spy holes and vaults and all the rest."

"Hormel," the brunette said softly, as if unsure and speaking his name would convince her.

"That's why he's been on my back recently. He knew who chased him through the house the other night. And he knows I'm after him for bushwhacking me. He shot my horse, took my money, cut down the Los Gatos sheriff— it's all his doing."

"How do you know he was the one out on the road?" asked Florabelle.

"I caught sight of him right after he'd sniped the sheriff. He wasn't decked out in the flour but he wore a mask with the identical markings as he's wearing now. Who else could it have been?"

". . . spirit will roam this house forever," Hormel finished.

Slocum hadn't caught the entire threat, but it obviously disturbed Sarah Winchester. The woman fidgeted nervously and her entire body shook in reaction.

"I'll do it. I can't have those evil spirits haunting me for the rest of my life. They killed William. They won't get me!"

"A gray eagle feather," Hormel intoned. "In the safe." Slocum took some small pleasure out of the way Hormel lisped through the split lip he had given him. He wished now that he'd finished the matter and snapped the son of a bitch's neck when he'd had the chance.

Slocum lifted his Colt, aiming carefully.

"John, no!" Florabelle hung on his arm. "You can't shoot him down in cold blood. You must turn him over to the sheriff."

"Hell I can't. He robbed me, he shot my horse." Slocum turned enough to keep Florabelle behind him as he raised his gun and cocked it. The woman's outburst had alerted Hormel that something had gone awry.

Although Slocum and Florabelle were partially hidden by the darkness, some glint off the gun barrel must have warned Hormel. Just as Slocum fired, the man-ghost dropped. Slocum saw wood splinters flying in the chamber. He'd missed.

"What's happening?" demanded Mrs. Winchester. She rose, hardly more than five feet tall, and leaned forward on her seance table. The small crystal ball wobbled, then rolled off its stand to smash into glassy shards on the floor.

"John," Florabelle begged.

He ignored her and moved out into the room, his Colt ready. Slocum fired again when he caught sight of a flash at the far end of the long, darkened room. Fragments from the war shield flew into the air, but Slocum knew he had again missed Hormel.

"What's the meaning of this?" shrieked Sarah Winchester. "Who are you? How dare you frighten the good spirits?"

Slocum kept his back to her and went hunting for Hormel. It was his turn to duck. A small movement in the corner of his eye alerted him to drop to his belly in time to avoid the thrusting war lance. A hard foot slammed into his side.

But this proved to be Hormel's undoing. The man lost his balance and tumbled over Slocum.

"Got you now, you thieving bastard!" said Slocum.

Hormel proved resourceful in the extreme. The mock ghost called out for Mrs. Winchester's benefit, "I am called! I must return to the spirit world instantly or be forever doomed to wander this house. Help me return!"

The woman helped her ghost guide. Slocum rolled onto

his back in time to see Mrs. Winchester opening a small hatch in the wall. Hormel dived head-first into the hole and vanished from sight, leaving behind both shield and war lance—and a white ring where the flour had rubbed off his body.

Even if he'd wanted, Slocum couldn't have gotten past Sarah Winchester in time to stop the foreman's escape.

Slocum saw that his opportunity to take Hormel had evaporated like mist in the sun.

Slocum rolled to his feet and burst past the red-robed woman. Florabelle tried to protest, to stop and speak with Mrs. Winchester. Slocum's strong arm caught the brunette around her trim waist and carried her back to the secret panel leading to the robe room. They bulled their way through the door, stumbled, regained balance, and kept running.

Behind, Slocum heard Mrs. Winchester screaming that she was being attacked by evil spirits.

Slocum cursed his bad luck, but came to realize that nothing had been lost. He knew for certain that Clarence Hormel moved through the mansion as the Indian ghost. Slocum almost recognized the need to prove his charges against Hormel. Gunning the man down wasn't the way to achieve justice; in this Florabelle had been right. Hormel would have to be turned over to Sheriff Thompson with enough proof to convict him.

But it had been so satisfying to have Hormel in the sights of his Colt, if only for an instant.

16

"Seen Hormel tonight?" Slocum asked Benny Buchanan. The other man turned from his work, wiped sweat from his forehead, and perched on the corner of a sawhorse before answering.

"Can't say that I have. You lookin' for him to shoot you in the back?"

"That hadn't occurred to me," Slocum lied, "but I figured that he'd be riding me especially hard since our fight. Haven't seen hide nor hair of him tonight."

"Can't say that I have, either." Buchanan took another swipe at his forehead. "You sure do pack a wallop. Glad I wasn't on the receivin' end of one of those punches. But you take care to watch your back. I ain't sayin' Hormel's a backshooter or anything like that, but he's an ornery son of a bitch. I seen him take down men twice his size."

"Maybe I ought to make my peace with him. Wouldn't want him to sneak up on me while I'm sleeping."

Buchanan cocked his head to one side and studied Slocum. The way his eyes narrowed showed that he didn't believe this lie for an instant. Slocum tried to look sincere about it but failed. He had to know if Hormel had it in for him after tonight. There was a chance that the Indian ghost didn't know who had been shooting at him in the seance room. Slocum knew that Hormel would have a good idea, but he couldn't go around gunning down everyone, if he was wrong.

"I'm gettin' damn tired of this job," said Buchanan. "Don't mind buildin' crazy rooms, but when we got to build 'em, then tear 'em down, now that's plumb loco."

The entire shift had been one of destruction. They had found a scribbled note telling them to tear down the walls in the room they had built less than a week before. Slocum thought this suspicious, but Buchanan shook his head and said that it happened several times a month. Mrs. Winchester ordered work to be done constantly, and it didn't matter to her if rooms went up or came down, as long as it confused the evil spirits trying to enter her house.

"You're lookin' thoughtful tonight, Slocum. What's burnin' away at your brain so much?"

"Mostly it's Hormel."

"He's a mean one, but unless I miss my guess, you're a sight meaner. He's the one what should be afraid of you." Buchanan paused, then added, "Carryin' around that six-shooter of yours like you been doin' is a mighty strong message. If you use it half as good as you use your fists, you must be a dead shot."

"I'm all right," Slocum said.

"Hormel's a good shot, too," said Buchanan. "Heard tell he was raised by Utes. Folks was killed when he was young. Somewhere in southwest Colorado, it was. The Utes took and raised him for almost five years before the white men got him back. That might explain why Hormel's such a strange fish."

Slocum's mind worked even harder at this. The war paint worn by the Indian ghost wasn't recognizable as Ute, but it could be. If Hormel had lived with the Indians, he would know of such matters. It also made sense that Hormel would consider the ghostly charade when he learned of Sarah Winchester's beliefs.

The lure of gold and jewels in the Winchester vaults, the knowledge of Utes, Mrs. Winchester's mystical certainty that Indian spirits haunted her—and a greedy man might do everything that Slocum now knew that Hormel had done.

But why ruin such a fine scheme with riding out and holding up stages on the Los Gatos road? Why shoot Slocum's horse from under him and then rob him? Even five hundred in greenbacks would be paltry compared to the loot Hormel could expect from a rich widow woman like Sarah Winchester. Why risk it all for a few extra dollars? Another thing that puzzled Slocum was the way the theft was accomplished. Road agents usually didn't like to change their style of doing their business.

But Slocum had seen the sniper who shot down the sheriff. The man was Hormel's size and he had worn a mask done up in the same pattern of war paint used by the Winchester mansion ghost.

There was no reason to believe Slocum's getting robbed and Sheriff Thompson being gunned down were isolated cases, or were done by different outlaws.

Slocum's head started to hurt. Everything pointed to Clarence Hormel. Hell, he *knew* Hormel was the Indian ghost.

He tried to forget it, but his brain refused to give up. He needed a way to convince the law that Hormel was guilty. And as Slocum worked it over, a plan developed. Slowly at first, then with greater enthusiasm, he pulled at the nails holding the studs in the walls. He ripped out two entire sections in the time it took Buchanan to do one—and Slocum hardly noticed.

The plan formed in his head, and it was a good one.

Slocum had gone off shift and dropped onto his bunk, waiting for Hormel. The foreman never showed up. In a way, Slocum wasn't surprised. The outlaw had to know his scheme was petering out. If he wanted to bilk Sarah Winchester out of a single dime he would have to do it tonight or lose any chance he had.

Slocum dozed fitfully all day, trying to conserve his strength, but also fearful that Hormel might take a shot at him through an open window. Once, he came awake, hammer back on the Colt, only to find Buchanan tromping heavily across the floor, knocking dust from his clothing as he went.

"Been out on guard duty for Yamaguchi," Buchanan said. "Go on back to sleep. I am." With that, Buchanan threw himself full-length on his bunk and was snoring loudly within minutes. Slocum took longer to go back to his half-awake, half-asleep state. But when the sun went down, he was up and ready to put his plan into action.

He crept from the bunkhouse. Buchanan still snored and half a dozen others on the night shift were tossing and turning, about ready to wake up and get some supper.

Slocum considered telling Florabelle of his plan, then

decided not to involve the woman. She might not approve of what had to be done, and whether or not she did, Florabelle would get in the way. Slocum wanted to take Hormel alive, but a man who'd been raised by the Utes might have other ideas.

Slocum sucked in the good, clean, cool night air as he made his way to the barn. He drew the Peacemaker and had it cocked and ready for action when he slipped inside. For a moment, he stood in the deep shadows just inside the door, waiting and listening. His eyes adjusted to the more intense darkness and he found the source of the small rustling noise that caught his attention.

To his right. He moved slowly, skillfully, making no sound. Slocum swung, gun level, ready to fire.

"Florabelle!" he exclaimed. The brunette sat in one stall, her skirts spread chastely around her, hands folded in her lap. She gave every indication of having been here for some time, patiently waiting.

"Good evening, John. I wondered when you would show up."

"It's dangerous being here," he said. "Hormel's got to get what he can from Mrs. Winchester tonight or lose any chance. He'd be expecting someone to ambush him here."

"I thought on that a while, John, and I decided it wasn't so. A man like Hormel knows these grounds and the house better'n anyone else. I asked some of the other maids and was told that he's worked here almost a year. A skilled carpenter with access to all the blueprints? He *knows* this house."

"So?"

"So I am sure that there are many other ways into the house. Hormel has no reason to use this entry point a second time, especially knowing that we discovered him here."

"You're saying that he'd get inside some other way?"

"Of course." Florabelle seemed pleased with herself, and Slocum had to admit she was probably right. Hormel was no fool. Their being in the seance room couldn't have been an accident; Hormel had to assume he'd been followed through the tunnel. Being seen entering in the barn was a likely conclusion—and Slocum hadn't made much secret of hunting him down, either. With Florabelle in the loft the night before and Slocum hanging about, Hormel had to know the barn would be too dangerous.

"You still took a chance."

"Yes," she said simply. "How about yourself, John Slocum? You're not taking a chance tonight? I know your mind as well as you do. You're going back into Mrs. Winchester's room to stop Hormel."

"It's a mite more complicated than that."

"You just want all the fun," Florabelle pouted.

"I've got the Colt. That makes it a damn sight less fun and more dangerous. I don't want you getting hurt."

Florabelle gave a tiny sigh. "Mrs. Murchison warned me of situations such as this. Men are all alike. You just don't want us womenfolk to have any excitement in our lives."

"Go on back to your room. You'll only be in the way."

"Very well, but at least let me help you."

"Help me?" asked Slocum, startled. "What do you mean?"

"I said I knew your mind better'n you did, John. And I do. You're not going to simply barge in on poor Mrs. Winchester again. She'd have a conniption fit right on the spot and you'd never be able to convince her of anything. No, you're going to do something sneakier, unless I miss my guess."

"You don't. If Hormel can pose as an Indian ghost, why

shouldn't there be a second one?"

"My thoughts exactly. Now sit yourself down and let me work on you. I took many drama courses in school and learned about makeup. If you're going to be an Indian ghost, I want you looking good—certainly more ghostly than Hormel. Such shoddy work, I do declare!"

Slocum skinned out of his shirt and let Florabelle begin applying flour to his body. She took a certain delight in finding places where it didn't want to stick. The brunette would run her lips lightly over the spot and then apply the flour. It tended to cake, but she found the most stimulating places to work on.

"Now for the war paint," she said, running a stick of charcoal over Slocum's flour-white face.

"Don't try to duplicate the lines," Slocum said. "Start under the left cheekbone, then go up slightly with three parallel marks. On the right cheek make only a single line."

"Why?"

"I think Hormel is using Ute design. This is Navajo." Florabelle said nothing to this, so Slocum explained. "Utes and Navajos don't get along well. Anything I can do to make Hormel just a tad uneasier, I'll try."

"You look positively . . . ghostly," she said, stepping back to study her handiwork.

Slocum had left his trousers on. These he smeared with charcoal to turn them jet black. He hung a knife on his belt and stuck the heavy Colt into his waistband at the small of his back.

"I've got to find the way into the secret tunnel," he said, "without doing too much damage to my makeup."

"Here, let me show you something." Florabelle eagerly dashed across the barn to the stall where Hormel had vanished the night before. She ran her hand along the top of the stall, yelped when she picked up a splinter in one finger, then went back to hunting. Slocum heard a sharp snap when Florabelle touched a certain portion of the wall.

A segment of floor pulled up and revealed a ladder down into a black hole.

"I didn't do any exploring down there," the brunette said, shuddering slightly. "I don't like caves, and there must be spiders and bugs."

"You shouldn't have gone this far," Slocum said. He bent and quickly kissed her, then dropped into the seemingly bottomless hole, hands on the ladder rungs before his feet found purchase. "Go on back to your room. This won't take long."

He mentally added, *One way or the other*.

"Good luck, John."

The trapdoor closed above him, leaving him in utter darkness. Slocum made his way along the earthen tunnel, one hand on the wall for balance and his feet moving in step-slide, step-slide fashion. He had the impression of being underground for weeks when he saw something ahead.

Eyes!

Slocum reached behind and whipped out the Colt, then relaxed. Those weren't eyes, they were spy holes opening onto a lighted room. He cautiously advanced and peered through the nearest hole into the kitchen. Two of the cooks sat at a long, narrow table playing cards and occasionally looking over their shoulders furtively to be certain Mrs. Winchester didn't catch them gambling.

Slocum went on through the tunnel until he found a spiraling staircase. This had to be the one they'd found the night before but hadn't explored. Step by step, Slocum went up. Past the first floor, past the second to the third. Pressing an ear against the door panel leading into the corridor, he waited for a few minutes until convinced no one lurked outside in ambush.

A brother to the shadows, Slocum slipped into the house from the secret stairway. His eyes had adjusted to lower levels of light; he had no trouble seeing clearly because the gas lamp flickered fitfully and cast only wan illumination in the corridor. He walked quickly to the room where he and Florabelle had entered Mrs. Winchester's seance chamber the night before. Slocum struggled with the sliding panel, then pulled it back into place.

Crouched down, he waited in the still darkness. Almost immediately he heard the swish of fabric. A spring lock snapped open and Sarah Winchester entered the seance room, her dark red robe dragging the floor as she walked. She hastily sat at the table. The smashed crystal ball had been replaced, he saw.

The woman began her invocation to get a spirit guide.

Slocum started to rise up and speak when he heard the floorboards creaking. Before he could react, Hormel made his presence known.

"Sarah Winchester!" the bogus ghost intoned. Hormel had chosen a spot in the room where a small window provided a modicum of light to shine off his flour coating. Slocum again marveled at how real such a simple disguise looked. For Mrs. Winchester, who believed in spirits, it must be all the more real.

"O Great and Gracious Spirit, I beseech you!" she cried.

"There is trouble. I am hunted by evil ones. I need immediate aid to drive away the cruel spirits who seek to harm us both."

"Anything!"

"Take the contents of the vault in the room that looks to the sunrise and place it in the center of the hallway outside."

"But why? How is this going to help?" asked the woman. Her suspicious tone told Slocum that Hormel would have to argue convincingly. He didn't.

Slocum knew that Hormel's trick of learning the safe combinations would have worked, given time. But Sarah Winchester's innate suspicion, even of friendly spirits, worked against him. Hormel had to risk more now if he wanted to succeed.

Slocum shot to his feet and cried, "Evil one! You seek to rob this woman of her fortune!"

Slocum took two quick steps forward and found a ray of light to spotlight his own flour and makeup. The look of shock on Hormel's face was worth the effort he'd gone through. Slocum didn't know if it was the presence of another ghost or if it was the pattern of the war paint. For a brief instant, Hormel might have actually believed he was confronting the ghost of a Navajo warrior.

The foreman recovered swiftly, giving up the masquerade. His hand flashed to a knife belted at his waist.

Slocum considered drawing his Colt and ending it. Then he smiled. He had bested Hormel once and it had felt good, damn good. And he did want to take the man alive to make him confess. Only in this way could Sheriff Thompson have a chance to bring Hormel to trial.

Slocum yanked out his own knife and advanced.

"Stop, wait, don't!" cried Mrs. Winchester.

The men locked in deadly embrace, each striving to gut the other. Around and around they spun, angling for advantage. Hormel might have been the stronger of the two, but Slocum was more agile and the better knife fighter. He turned suddenly, caught Hormel off balance, and drew a red streak across the man's belly. Hormel yelped in pain, backing off before Slocum could recover.

"He is a fake, a fraud. He sought only to deceive you.

Ghosts don't bleed," said Slocum. He spoke to Sarah Winchester, but he never took his eyes off Hormel.

Knife met knife, sending more sparks flying into the darkened room. Slocum lifted his leg in time to block a knee to the groin, then jerked Hormel around and sent the man slamming hard into a wall.

"Evil! You're both evil spirits!" cried Mrs. Winchester. "Begone! You are banished from my home! Don't ever return!"

Hormel took this as his chance to run. Slocum expected him to try to recover his fallen knife. Hormel bolted for a door and was through it before Slocum realized he was letting the man escape.

Slocum took off after him, knife in hand. Hormel was unarmed now. It ought to be easier to catch him, except for the foreman's knowledge of the house. He had vanished from sight in the span of a hurried heartbeat.

Slocum held back a curse. He dropped to the floor and pressed his ear against the boards. From inside the seance room came Sarah Winchester's frantic movements, but Slocum detected the slap-slap of bare feet farther down the hall. He sprinted ahead, hot on Hormel's heels.

Slocum almost died because of his haste.

"Got you, you son of a bitch. You ruined everything for me with the old woman. Now you're gonna die!"

Slocum hadn't considered the possibility of Hormel having another weapon hidden in the house. He now faced the sweat-streaked man holding a sixshooter in his hand.

Old reflexes took over. Slocum didn't consciously think of what he did—he simply reacted. His hand came up and the knife went cartwheeling toward Hormel. The throw was clumsy and poorly aimed. The handle instead of the point hit Hormel in the arm, deflecting the shot just enough to save Slocum's life.

Slocum dived into a room, hand groping for his own Colt. When Hormel appeared in the doorway, Slocum got off two quick shots. The gasp of pain told him one slug had found a home—but he was off target. Hormel darted away again.

Slocum got a third shot at the disappearing ghost. He missed.

Through the upper story of the house, they chased one another, taking potshots. Slocum saw a tiny trickle of red seeping from where he'd creased Hormel's upper arm. It would hurt like hell, but it wasn't serious. It didn't even slow the other man down.

Slocum avoided the splinters from a doorway as Hormel fired a wild shot in his direction. Then Slocum had his chance. Hormel had gone into a room without another exit. Slocum spun around in a crouch, Colt cocked and ready for action. His finger tightened and the hammer fell on an empty cylinder.

Hormel vented a bull-throated roar and charged, his pistol swinging like a club. Slocum realized that Hormel was out of ammunition, too, but that didn't help him any. They crashed together. For an instant Slocum stood against the onslaught, then he fell backwards.

Glass shattered. Slocum winced as a million tiny knives cut at his bare back. Then both he and Hormel fell through the air. Slocum saw triumph flare on Hormel's face. When they landed he would be on top.

Slocum tried to twist to one side, to avoid having Hormel's full weight crush him. He only partly succeeded. They fell side by side onto a table in the middle of a first-floor foyer.

Struggling for advantage, they both sat up. The impact of cascading water drove them both back to the tabletop amid a mixture of water, flour, and blood. Slocum recovered before Hormel and looked up. On a second-story balcony, the Chinese butler stood silently, a Winchester Model '73 in hand, and aimed at them.

Slocum put up his hands. Beside him, Clarence Hormel did the same.

17

"I should have him shoot both of you where you stand," Miss Merriam said, anger turning her face into a dark mask. She trembled with wrath. "Get them into the study. And be quick about it," she ordered the butler. "I don't want to disturb my aunt."

"He jumped me!" exclaimed Hormel. "He—"

"Be quiet, Mr. Hormel. I do not for an instant believe that Mr. Slocum is solely at fault." She eyed the flour-covered, war-paint-bedecked foreman with obvious displeasure. "What sort of prank you two were playing on my aunt remains to be seen, but it will certainly be cause for immediate dismissal."

Slocum saw Hormel relax and a slight smile cross his lips. Losing his job was the farthest thing from his mind. If he had the chance, Hormel could be on horseback and a hundred miles away before dawn came on the day after this one.

The silent Chinese butler covered them from the balcony as they went into the study. When Hormel tensed to make good his escape, Slocum turned and swung with all his might. His fist sank wrist-deep in the foreman's belly. By the time the butler appeared with rifle in hand, Hormel had fought enough air back into his lungs to gasp.

"Son of a bitch! You saw what he did!"

"Be quiet, Mr. Hormel. This is a serious matter," said Margaret Merriam. "I must protect my aunt, no matter how much that I feel she is being foolish with this spirit business she dotes on. You and Mr. Slocum are the cause of great unrest in the Winchester mansion, not the least of it confined to my aunt."

"It's serious," said Slocum. "I want you to send for Sheriff Thompson over in Los Gatos. He's the man to settle this. Hormel tried to bilk Mrs. Winchester out of the contents of several of her vaults by pretending to be a ghost."

Margaret Merriam motioned Hormel to silence. "One may speak at a time. Since Mr. Slocum has already started, he can have his say. Then you may respond to his allegations. Go on." Her eyes bored into Slocum's green, unwavering gaze.

"Thank you, Miss Merriam. Using his Indian-ghost outfit, Hormel tried to dupe your aunt into opening one safe at a time. Using his knowledge as construction foreman, he spied on her when she worked the safes and got the combinations."

"My aunt *has* been going on about evil spirits and white feathers in her safes," agreed Miss Merriam.

"He's also responsible for the thefts. The silver service,

the gems pulled from their setting, then—"

"I never did any such thing!" shouted Hormel.

Margaret Merriam motioned Slocum to silence and gave the nod to Hormel.

"He's responsible!" cried Hormel."He's the thief. I only dressed up like this to try to catch him in the act. And I did! My record here speaks for itself. He's come in and tried to—"

"That answers one question," the woman said. "The Indian ghost appeared long before Mr. Slocum came to work here. I am inclined to think *you* are the culprit, but we need more definite proof."

Before Slocum could speak, Florabelle Jackson's high, clear voice cut through the room. "Miss Merriam, I have proof that Clarence Hormel is a thief. I saw him one night dressed up as he is now. Mr. Slocum wanted to catch him in the act and tried to copy his charade."

"What is your interest in this, Miss Jackson?"

"I saw Hormel trying to open one of the vaults and failing. He's tried to get me in bad with you and Mrs. Winchester at every turn since that night."

"He did accuse you of theft," the secretary said. "Are you so accusing him now?"

"I am. Have his quarters searched. Something he's stolen from Mrs. Winchester must be there."

"Go on. You won't find a damn thing," growled Hormel.

Miss Merriam went to a speaking tube, blew into it, and gave curt commands. "It will take a few minutes, but Mr. Yamaguchi is a thorough man. If there is anything to find, he will find it."

"This was only a prank," said Hormel. "You can fire me for that, but you've got nothing else on me."

No one spoke. Hormel subsided, glowering. Now and

then he glanced at the butler, but the stolid Chinese held the rifle in rock-steady hands. Leaving without him getting off at least one shot would be impossible. For his part, Slocum was content to wait, but he was still worried.

Searching Hormel's quarters would turn up nothing. The foreman was too clever to leave evidence around.

Slocum's heart almost exploded from his chest when Yamaguchi entered. In the gardener's hand was a heavily laden pillow case that looked all too familiar.

"This was stolen," Yamaguchi said. "I recognize this serving tray." He dropped the tray and several forks onto the oak table. A small pouch of gemstones followed. "He very clever in concealment, but I am cleverer in searching." Yamaguchi bowed slightly and stepped back, arms crossed and dark eyes fixed on Hormel.

"They planted that. The two of them!"

"We will summon Sheriff Thompson. The evidence is clear. Mr. Yamaguchi, place our former construction foreman in detention. The room behind the sawmill should do nicely until the sheriff can arrive and take custody of his prisoner."

"No, he's responsible. He did it. He—"

Yamaguchi reached out and took Hormel's arm in a deceptively gentle hold. Whatever he did, the man stopped struggling suddenly and walked along on tiptoe, pain etched on his features.

"You are absolved of any crime, Mr. Slocum. But because of all that has happened, I believe it would be in everyone's best interest if you were no longer employed by Mrs. Winchester in any capacity. You will be given a full month's severance pay. That is more than fair, given the unusual circumstances."

"I understand," Slocum said. He wasn't about to argue his way into a long, drawn-out legal hearing.

"There's something else," said Florabelle. "Hormel is also the—" Slocum took her by the arm and squeezed hard enough to cut off her words. He shook his head slightly, silently warning her not to mention their belief that Clarence Hormel was also the road agent who had shot down the sheriff.

"I know what you wanted to ask, my dear," said Miss Merriam. "Since you were not directly connected with this evening's unfortunate prank, you may retain your position in the household staff."

"Thank you," said Slocum, almost dragging Florabelle from the room.

In the hall, Florabelle spun about, furious. "You should have let me tell her about him being the outlaw. Why'd you stop me?"

"Let's leave all that for Sheriff Thompson," said Slocum. "No need to burden Miss Merriam with too much accusing right now. She's had a hard night."

Florabelle smiled crookedly as she ran her fingers over his sweaty, flour-streaked chest. "Looks like you've had a hard night, too."

"It could get harder," he said. He sucked in his breath when Florabelle checked to see how hard it might be. Arms around each other, they went to her bedroom, not caring who saw them now.

"This is going to be tricky, Miss Merriam," said Sheriff Thompson. The man's complexion looked better than the last time Slocum had seen him. The sheriff was gaining strength daily. He seemed in his element before the large crowd of employees gathered in front of the mansion. Most stood in a wide semicircle, not wanting to get too close, but too curious not to press in. When Benny Buchanan rode up, finished with his guard duty for the morning, this broke the spell. The others came in so close that less than a pace separated them from the sheriff and his prisoner.

"We can't involve Mrs. Winchester, is that it?" Sheriff Thompson went on. He eyed Buchanan and the fact that he toted a gun—the only other one besides Slocum and himself. Then his attention went back to the matter at hand.

"Correct, Sheriff."

"But we have enough evidence, if this young lady's willing to testify. And Mr. Yamaguchi, of course. His testimony is central to any case, even if a judge's not likely to listen much to a chink."

"They will so testify. As long as Mrs. Winchester does not have to appear in court. She refuses to be seen in public."

"I know that she's a mite on the shy side." Sheriff Thompson started to say something more, then bit it back. "All right. Get that jasper into the carriage. Those manacles ought to hold him till we get to the jailhouse."

Heavy leg and wrist manacles held Hormel firmly. A half dozen of the crowd obliged the sheriff by throwing Hormel into the back of the carriage. The man sat sullenly, finally realizing his thieving at the Winchester mansion was at an end.

"Sheriff," Florabelle spoke up. She glared at Slocum, as if daring him to speak. The brunette had wanted to declare her knowledge of the road agent's identity in front of Miss Merriam the night before. Now she would do it for the sheriff's benefit.

"There's something else, Sheriff," Florabelle said. "You know the road agent who's been giving you fits?"

Thompson touched the spot on his chest where the two slugs had entered. He said nothing. He simply stared at her.

"I know who is responsible."

Thompson turned and looked toward the carriage. Hormel hadn't changed his hunched-over posture. He was totally beaten.

"You mean we got the cat what's responsible for eating two birds?" Sheriff Thompson asked.

Slocum turned to his right and looked around the circle of men gathered to watch their foreman being taken away. He faced Benny Buchanan squarely and said to Florabelle, "Go on, Miss Jackson. Tell the sheriff who's the road agent. The one who shot him, who's been robbing the Wells, Fargo stages, the one who robbed me and shot my horse."

Something in Slocum's tone made Florabelle hesitate.

"Go on, miss. Who is it?" asked Thompson. "It *is* that owlhoot you're talkin' about, ain't it?"

"Not Hormel," said Slocum. "Someone else. There were two thieves at work in the Santa Clara Valley." His cold green eyes locked with Buchanan's. "I always thought it was downright stupid for Hormel to jeopardize everything here. There might be thousands in Mrs. Winchester's vaults. Why rile up the countryside and maybe lose his chance at all that money with road-agenting?"

"Why?" asked the sheriff.

"Because Hormel worked strictly inside the mansion. Someone else worked the road, robbing and killing. Someone Mr. Yamaguchi sent out to protect the perimeter of the estate. Someone who had the chance to slip away often with his sixshooter and a rifle and not raise suspicion here. Someone who fed me information that would point toward Hormel being the road agent."

Slocum's hand flashed for his Colt at exactly the same instant Buchanan went for his pistol. Two deafening reports rang out as one.

Slocum beat Buchanan by a fraction of a second. One

shot had gone into the ground; the other hadn't. Buchanan started to say something, reached to his chest, and dropped his gun doing so. He finally croaked out, "I always knowed you was a damn sight meaner'n Hormel."

Buchanan fell face forward to lie in the dust twitching feebly. In a few seconds even this twitching ceased.

"Buchanan?" whispered Florabelle. "But I thought . . ."

"He was a cunning man," said Slocum. "And I even liked him." He took a deep breath, and said, "But damn it, he shouldn't have killed my horse."

"This looks to be one red-letter day for the entire valley," said Sheriff Thompson. "A sneak thief posing as an Injun ghost and the bushwhacker what's been bedeviling the whole countryside."

Thompson walked over to Slocum and thrust out his hand. "You don't follow the law, but damn it, son, you get things done right."

Slocum took his hand and shook it.

Miss Merriam, pale of face and holding a frilly lace handkerchief to her trembling lips, cleared her throat to get the sheriff's attention. "Sir, it is my understanding that there is a reward on this man's head. Is that not so?"

"Well, yes, ma'am, there is. A hundred dollars."

"Two hundred," spoke up Mr. Yamaguchi. "I can read your posters. They hang everywhere. The wind blows them into my gardens and I must pick them up."

"Two hundred, that's right," said Thompson.

The sheriff looked from Miss Merriam to Slocum and back. He came to his decision in a hurry. "Since it looks as if the crook was brought to justice on Mrs. Winchester's property, I suppose it's only fittin' that she be given the reward. Is that all right, Miss Merriam?"

"Imminently so, Sheriff."

"But John was the one—"

Slocum quieted Florabelle's protest. He didn't care who got the reward. Let Thompson keep it. Let Miss Merriam have it. Let her divvy it up among the entire staff. It made no nevermind to him. He was satisfied having evened the score. He wasn't going to get his money back, and the horse was buzzard meat a long time back, but Buchanan wouldn't be doing that to any other luckless travelers. That was good enough.

"Best be gettin' my prisoner into Los Gatos," said Thompson. "I'll get the reward money out to you within a week."

Miss Merriam and the butler accompanied the sheriff as far as the front gates.

"John?" asked Florabelle.

"I got to go. That was part of the deal we made last night with Miss Merriam. Remember? It's for the best." Slocum hoped that Florabelle wouldn't beg to be allowed to come along with him. His kind of life wasn't for her. She belonged in these rich, comfortable settings. One day, he had no doubt, she would work her way up to a position of wealth and responsibility, if she stayed with Miss Merriam and Mrs. Winchester.

"I don't know how to say this, John." She stood on tiptoe and kissed him quickly. She took a deep breath and rushed on, "I want to stay. Life's been hard for me since my parents died. There's . . . stability here in the mansion. Can you understand that?" Her brown eyes welled with tears.

"I can." He kissed her lightly, then swung into the saddle. The swayback mare protested, but Slocum wasn't in any hurry. He kicked and got the horse moving.

At the gate, Miss Merriam signaled for him to stop.

"Yes, ma'am?"

The woman motioned. The Chinese butler handed over

a white envelope. Slocum looked inside. It held five twenty-dollar bills.

"Half of the reward for Mr. Buchanan. I will see that Miss Jackson gets the other half."

"This is in the way of a bribe?"

"We don't expect to see you here again, Mr. Slocum. You have the reward and you have your severance pay. Good day, and have a pleasant journey."

John Slocum rode on. The heavy wooden portals slammed behind him. He heard the sound of hammers until he got to San Jose.

JAKE LOGAN

___ 07139-1	**SOUTH OF THE BORDER**	$2.50
___ 07567-2	**SLOCUM'S PRIDE**	$2.50
___ 07382-3	**SLOCUM AND THE GUN-RUNNERS**	$2.50
___ 07494-3	**SLOCUM'S WINNING HAND**	$2.50
___ 08382-9	**SLOCUM IN DEADWOOD**	$2.50
___ 08279-2	**VIGILANTE JUSTICE**	$2.50
___ 08189-3	**JAILBREAK MOON**	$2.50
___ 08392-6	**SIX GUN BRIDE**	$2.50
___ 08076-5	**MESCALERO DAWN**	$2.50
___ 08539-6	**DENVER GOLD**	$2.50
___ 08644-X	**SLOCUM AND THE BOZEMAN TRAIL**	$2.50
___ 08742-5	**SLOCUM AND THE HORSE THIEVES**	$2.50
___ 08773-5	**SLOCUM AND THE NOOSE OF HELL**	$2.50
___ 08791-3	**CHEYENNE BLOODBATH**	$2.50
___ 09088-4	**THE BLACKMAIL EXPRESS**	$2.50
___ 09111-2	**SLOCUM AND THE SILVER RANCH FIGHT**	$2.50
___ 09299-2	**SLOCUM AND THE LONG WAGON TRAIN**	$2.50
___ 09212-7	**SLOCUM AND THE DEADLY FEUD**	$2.50
___ 09342-5	**RAWHIDE JUSTICE**	$2.50
___ 09395-6	**SLOCUM AND THE INDIAN GHOST**	$2.50